THE KINSMEN UNIVERSE

ILONA ANDREWS

The Kinsmen Universe

Ebook ISBN: 9781641970693
KDP Print ISBN: 9798425723543
IS Print ISBN: 9781641971966

Silent Blade

Ebook ISBN: 9781641970617

Silver Shark

Ebook ISBN: 9780983954613

NYLA Publishing

121 W 27th St., Suite 1201, New York, NY 10001

http://www.nyliterary.com

SILENT BLADE

Chapter 1

In the course of space colonization, there arose a need for humans with enhanced abilities. Men and women who could survive harsh conditions, who were superb warriors, gifted hunters, and brilliant scientists.

Some enhancements were technological in nature: an array of implants with various functions. Their effect ended with the death of the person who carried them. Other improvements were biological and these enhanced capabilities persisted, lingering in the bloodline, changing and mutating into new abilities in the offspring of the original carrier. It was quickly realized that the advantage of these biological enhancements lay in their exclusivity. Thus, the biologically enhanced united and shut down all further biological modification.

Collectively known as kinsmen, these exceptional beings gave rise to several dozen families, which now form the financial elite of the colonized planets. The kinsmen strictly control their numbers and their loyalty to their families is absolute. Like the Sicilian mafia families and feuding Corsican clans of the old planet, the kinsmen exist in tense competition with each other. It is that competition that rules the economy, begins and ends wars, and drags human civilization to greater technological and scientific progress.

Chapter 2

"Place your hands on the panel in front of you." The bodyguard, in a sleek grey uniform of Canopus Inc., nodded at the plasti-steel console that sprouted from the luxurious rug like a mushroom on a thin metal stalk.

Meli smiled. Four high-caliber gun turrets swiveled on their mounts on the ceiling, tracking her every movement as she rested her fingers on the panel, a thin bracelet sliding down on her right wrist. She had already passed through a number of metal detectors and submitted to a search and a chemical sniffer. Only one final test remained.

Light slid along her fingertips as a complex array of scanners feverishly assessed her temperature, heat, and chemical emissions, sampled the composition of her sweat and oil on her fingertips, and probed her body for foreign influences. A long moment stretched. A calm female voice with the crisp unaccented pronunciation of the computer announced, "Implant scan, class A through C, negative. Biological modification negative."

The guard relaxed slightly. The tense line of his shoulders eased. A person like her had no chance against a bodyguard equipped with a combat implant that sharpened his reflexes and increased his strength.

"You may step down," he permitted. "Follow me."

She walked behind him to the large wooden door polished to an amber gleam. Maruvian pine, unthinkable luxury. The guard tapped a code on his wrist. The door slid aside, revealing a second, steel partition. The steel wall split in half and parted. Meli strode into a spacious office. The door whispered shut behind her.

Three people waited in the office: an older man behind a desk cut from a single block of malachite, and two bodyguards, a woman and a man, both lean and sharp, positioned at the walls on opposite sides of her.

She smiled at them as well.

The man behind the desk leaned forward slightly. Agostino Canopus, thirty-eight, a kinsman, fourth son of Vierra Canopus, Arbitrator Second Class. Of average height, he sat with the easy authority of a man completely confident in his position. His hair, a dark copper, was cut and styled with artful precision. His skin was perfect. His eyes, two dark chunks of green, fastened on her. In a split second she was evaluated, measured and approved.

"Sit down." Agostino indicated a plain stool bolted to the floor with a casual sweep of his hand.

Meli sat.

"You came here to become a retainer of Canopus family," he said. "Why?"

"Power."

In the financial world, where most disputes were decided by arbitration, the arbitrators wielded unprecedented influence.

Agostino nodded. The answer seemed to satisfy him. "Your test scores are exceptional."

She accepted the compliment with a nod. "So is my reaction time."

His eyebrows came together. "What…"

She leapt off the chair. Obeying her mental command, a long ribbon of transparent green whipped from the narrow bracelet on her wrist. The ene-ribbon slashed the female bodyguard, whipped across the door, and kissed the male bodyguard across the chest.

Before Agostino's lips shaped the next word, Meli sat back onto the chair. Behind her two bodies slid apart, cleaved in two. The air smelled of fried electronics. She had disabled the control panel on the door.

Agostino surveyed the door. "You're a melder."

"Yes."

Melders like her were an extremely rare commodity. The mutation that permitted her to operate an energy ribbon came along once in every fifteen million, and most possessing it never discovered their abilities. In the world of combat implants and biochemical modifications, melders were the extraordinary natural-born freaks.

Agostino leaned back, one leg over the other, pleating his long fingers on his knee. "What's this about?"

"The Galdes family sends its regards."

Ten days ago he had presided over the arbitration between Galdes and Morgans. He'd ruled in favor of Morgans, finding no wrongdoing in the hostile takeover of Galdes's Valemia Inc.

"It was a fair arbitration," Agostino said.

"You've falsified the evidence." She kept her voice calm and pleasant. "You've altered the earnings estimates for the third and fourth quarters and assisted in hiding of Morgans' assets prior to takeover, creating an appearance of weakness. Your actions irreparably damaged the prestige of Galdes family and cut their income by one twelfth. You drove Arani Galdes, former CEO of Valemia, to commit suicide."

He didn't miss a beat. "Nobody can blame me for her death."

"I can," she told him.

"Ah." He inclined his head in a shallow bow. "So it's personal. Your retina scans do not trace back to Galdes. You aren't a kinsman. Why take a suicide so close to heart? Was she your lover?"

"My cousin."

His eyebrows crept up. "You're an excise."

He turned the word into an expletive, saying it the way one might mutter "cursed" or "leper". Even after twelve years it still stung a little. For a kinsman, family meant everything. Nothing could be worse than being disowned and cut off.

"Of course." Agostino snapped his fingers. "Your family cast you out, so you can commit atrocities on their behalf, and none of your actions can be traced back to them. You still have fond feelings for your cousin. My apologies. I didn't seek her death."

His gestures grew animated. She could almost feel the wheels turning in his head. He thought he saw a crack in her armor. Meli sighed.

"Your sacrifice is admirable. But I could offer you so much more. Your parents, your siblings, they threw you aside. What kind of family does that? Don't you want revenge?"

"It was my choice."

He stared at her, stunned. "You chose…? Why?"

She reached into her business suit and produced a thin sheet of plasti-paper. On it a young dark-haired woman laughed, wearing a crown of flowers. Meli slid the plastic across the table to him.

"What's this?"

"My cousin Arani. I wanted you to see her before you died."

"Reconsider!"

"You're my last kill," she told him. "After you, I will retire."

His face snapped into a hard mask. "There are six guards outside that door, not including automatic defenses. Even if you kill me, you'll never get out alive."

She gave him a bright smile as the ene-ribbon whipped from her wrist. She was still smiling when the top half of his skull slid to the floor.

NO MATTER THE HOUR, no matter the circumstance, Angel always looked perfect. Debonair in his tailored rust jerkin, with crispness to his lines and inborn poise so many spent years training to mimic, he seemed the very essence of a kinsman. His hair was a soft brown streaked with copper, his face was amiable and handsome, and his eyes were dark, just like hers. When he smiled from the display, it was as if the sun had risen. Fortunately, Meli had long ago become immune to his charm. After all, she had seen him in diapers.

"No more jobs," she told him. "I've retired." Two months had passed since Agostino Canopus died on the marble floor of his office. She liked her quiet and the sense of liberation retirement brought. No more jobs. No more death.

On the screen her brother leaned forward. "This is a personal request, Meli. From Father."

Meli closed her eyes. Angel had interrupted her morning exercise and since his call wasn't an emergency, she saw no reason not to continue. Around her the small house lay quiet, serene in the light of the early morning. A delicate lemony scent of brugmansia floated through the open screen door. She was aware of minute noises: water gurgling in the pipes, two bees buzzing in the small garden on her right, a faint whistling of the draft generated by the climate control system…

"Please, do him this favor."

"I'm done, Angel," she murmured. "We've spoken of this. The family has no right to ask me."

"Father knows that. Believe me, he wouldn't request this of you unless the need was dire."

She said nothing. Angel, while diplomatic, suffered from an eloquent man's malady—faced with silence, he felt compelled to fill it, even when it was in his best interests to keep his mouth shut.

Moments dripped by. Angel cleared his throat.

"Raban, Incorporated has dropped the price of the condenser units to below fifteen thousand standard dollars. It's a calculated move to edge out the competition. The condenser production is still the main source of our revenue. We can't underbid them. We can't even match them. The profit margin is too narrow for us to survive. They can take a loss, but we don't have the reserves to ride it out. We're a small family. We'll go bankrupt. And you know what happens to families that go bankrupt."

Without funds, a family couldn't pay its soldiers. The competition in New Delphi was too cut-throat for the family without soldiers to survive for long. The city housed twenty-one kinsman families of note, the metropolis divided between them like slices of a pie, in both economic and geographic sense. The Galdes' slice was rather small, but their soldiers were renowned for their expertise and loyalty. Their martial prowess was what had kept the family afloat this long.

"Please, Meli. You're still a Galdes. Even if you did retire."

Why did she feel guilt? She owed them nothing. She'd spent twelve years murdering on their behalf. She just wanted to be free now. Free and alone. Her father knew this. She'd made it abundantly clear during their last communication.

She didn't bend her rules, as the family learned the first time they tried to force her to kill a target without a sufficient reason. This job had to be special. Something she could refuse.

The curiosity got the better of her. "Who is the target?"

"Does this mean it's a yes?"

Meli sighed softly. "The target, Angel."

She supposed it had something to do with Raban, Inc., but she had excised herself from Galdes family years ago. Their business dealings remained a mystery to her. She had no idea who owned Raban, Inc.

She heard the barely audible click as Angel tapped the keys on his end of the screen.

A faint tug on her senses from the left. She didn't hear it, didn't see it, but felt it with some innate sixth sense, or perhaps an imperceptible combination of all five.

Meli struck.

Her eyes were still closed, but in her mind she clearly saw a ribbon of transparent green snapping from the bracelet on her hand. She felt the energy sear the target and smelled fried electronics.

"Good God," Angel said.

She opened her eyes in time to see the manta ray shaped disk of interceptor crash to the floor in a smoking ruin. Quiet and equipped with small caliber cannon, robotic interceptor units had long become a favorite in security. Their state of the art sensory systems ensured that they located intruders quickly and the absolute silence of their flight made their detection nearly impossible until their ammunition bit the back of the target's neck. She made it a point to kill at least one a month, to relieve tension and practice her strike on a moving target. It helped her stay sharp.

"It always rattles me when you do that," Angel said. "Here is the file."

A small icon ignited in the corner of the screen, indicating a downloaded file available for viewing. He hesitated. "I think you might enjoy this one. A bit of poetic justice, one might say. Give it a thought, Meli. Please. For me."

Angel touched his fingertips to his mouth, pressed them to his forehead, and bowed his head. The screen turned neutral grey, signaling the end of transmission.

Meli sighed. "Open file."

The icon grew to fill the screen with a facsimile of a manila folder. The folder opened. A picture of a man looked at her. Ice burst at the base of her neck and slid down her spine.

Celino Carvanna.

Two hours later Meli sat in the garden. Around her, dahlias bloomed in a dazzling display of a hundred shades. The delicate pink of Adelaide Fontane, the white frilly Aspen, the gaudy riot of orange that was Bodacious and her favorite, the Arabian Night, its sharpened petals a deep intense red of a Burgundy wine.

Beyond the small plot lay a narrow street, typical to Old Town, where streets were narrow, houses old, property values low, and residents still kept an occasional garden. Beyond the street lay a throughway. If she rose and approached the fence, she would see the steady current of aerials gliding through the air. A left turn on the throughway would bring her to the heart of New Delphi's financial district. A right would take her to the Terraces, where tourist shops and cafes catered to the upscale clientele eager for a touch of the "old planet" and the memories of provinces that lay beyond the city.

The city was the center of the South, the technological and economical hub of the subcontinent. Divided into territories between kinsmen, it served as their battleground. But those who had grown up in the provinces surrounding New Delphi never forgot their true home.

Meli had bought the house for the garden and filled it with dahlias, permitting only a few brugmansias and two pink silk trees for fragrance. It was her bright, cheerful haven, her little celebration of life and color, and affirmation of her own humanity. Her proof that she could nurture life as well as take it.

The file lay on her lap, downloaded into her notebook. She had read it, committing every word to memory. She had printed Celino's photograph. His face was a glossy smoothness underneath her fingertips.

She moved her hand and looked down on the god of her adolescence. He hadn't changed as much as she expected. The years had sharpened his face, honing his features with a lethal precision. A perfectly carved square jaw. A crisply defined nose with a small bump. His cheekbones protruded, the cheeks beneath them hollowed, making the contours of his face more pronounced. His eyebrows, two thick black lines, combined with the stubborn set of his wide, narrow-lipped mouth, gave his face a grim, menacing air. But it was the eyes that elevated his appearance from merely harsh to dangerous.

Dark grey, they matched the fabled bluish steel of Ravager firearms. Perceptive, powerful, they betrayed an intellect sharp enough to draw blood but revealed no emotion. Not even a minute glimpse of his inner self. She vividly remembered staring into their depths, trying to gauge what he felt for her, if anything, and finding only a hard opaque wall.

Every time she looked into those eyes, a jolt of adrenaline tore through her.

Meli forced herself to look at him again, trying to separate herself from the adolescent flutter of her pulse. That flutter, the slight pain in her chest, the rapid chill, all that was but a bitter memory of a little foolish girl, hardly more than a child. Her little foolish hopes and dreams had long turned to dust.

She had to evaluate him for what he was—a target.

In her mind a younger Celino sprang from her memories: handsome, tall, with a lazy, self-indulgent smile, standing on a verandah with a short blade in his hand, inviting the party guests to throw polymer drink cans at him. He was barely seventeen then. He looked incredible poised against the backdrop of the flower beds that gave the province of Dahlia its name. As a barrage of the multicolored containers hit him, he sliced at them in a blur, severing them with his blade. When he was done, the tile around him was drenched. Celino, on the other hand, remained perfectly dry.

Carvannas had a reputation for their knife skills, superb even among the kinsmen.

The man who looked at her from the photograph now wouldn't show off. Tempered by a decade and a half in the kinsmen family feuds, he would watch, calculating the odds, until the right moment came, and then he would seize it without hesitation and squeeze out every advantage. He had survived four known assassination attempts and likely a dozen or more that remained secret. She tapped the notebook screen, calling up the only recorded attempt. She had viewed it twice already.

The premiere of Gigolo. A brightly lit street. Red carpet stretching into the mouth of Miranda Theater. Adoring crowds shouting their worship at the stars and their escorts.

A sleek, bullet-shaped aerial slid up to the ropes. The door swung up. A metal step unfurled from the underside of the vehicle, permitting the passengers to exit in comfort. Celino stepped out. Tall, lean, and overwhelmingly masculine in the traditional

Carvanna black doublet stretched by his broad shoulders. He had matured well. Too well, Meli reflected.

He bent lightly, offering his hand, and immediately feminine fingers rested in his palm. A woman stepped out. She wore a glittering silvery sari that stopped a shade short of vulgar. In spiky heels, she stood only a couple of inches shorter than Celino, six two to his six four. A fountain of blonde hair spilled down her back all the way past her butt.

Celino led her down the carpet. They seemed perfectly matched—her glamorous light to his brooding darkness. A painful needle pierced Meli's chest. Old dreams, she reminded herself.

She sensed the attack a moment before it came. Celino's head jerked as the crowd on the right erupted and four men dashed at him. The magnetic disruptors installed by theater security made any metal projectiles unusable, and the attackers opted for dark red monomolecule blades.

Celino thrust his date behind him with a powerful shove and attacked so quickly, he blurred. He was preternaturally fast. Meli tapped the screen, slowing the recording by twenty-five percent. He held a simple metal knife. His swipe drew a bright red gash down the first attacker's throat—beautifully done. A vertical gash opened a bigger hole in the carotid without slowing down the strike. It was nearly impossible to hit the artery that way—like aiming at a piece of lubricated IV drip dancing around in the wind. Meli had factored in the enhanced strength and speed, but Celino seemed to have enhanced reflexes as well. Or perhaps a targeting implant. Or both.

The second cut grazed the second attacker's arm pit, severing another vein. The third assailant received a sideways swipe to the kidneys. That strike took a quarter of a second longer than Celino had planned. She saw him change his strategy in mid-move, hammering a kick to the fourth man's neck. She rewound half a second, slowed the feed to half speed, and watched Celino's black boot connect with the man's neck. She couldn't hear the telltale crunch, but she saw the man's neck line jerk sharply. Celino's kick had broken the vertebrae of his attacker.

She shut down the notebook. In a purely physical confrontation, Celino would kill her. She had absolutely no doubt of that. She was a small woman—he towered over her by a foot, outweighed her by at least eighty pounds of hard muscle, and he had enhancements she couldn't match. Judging from Celino's performance, very few people would be able to match him blow by blow. Add to it bodyguards, who always accompanied him. And Marcus. One couldn't forget Marcus. Only one generation removed from old planet, Marcus was ill-suited to traditional enhancements. Instead he had done horrible things to his body in the name of service. A walking poison, he killed with a mere touch. Celino had saved him years ago and Marcus was devoted to Celino like a dog.

To kill Celino Carvanna, she would have to get close to him and separate him from his guards.

Father was right. None of the people at Galdes disposal could take out Celino Carvanna. In fact, of all the millions that inhabited New Delphi, she alone was uniquely qualified to take him on.

Father, in his wisdom, also reasoned that she would do it. If not for the sake of Galdes, then for the sake of sliding the tomb stone atop her broken heart. He believed she would hate Celino Carvanna. After all, Celino had humiliated the Galdes family. He ruined her life, obliterating her future. Of course, she had to hate him.

Meli recalled the file. Celino chose to oversee a number of projects for the Carvannas, including Raban, Inc. and Sunlight Development. He was active and ruthless, and his leadership brought his family to its prominence. He made the Carvanna millions. For all practical purposes, he was the Carvanna family. His death would plunge his clan into chaos and destroy the value of their stock.

Angel had managed to obtain Celino's calendar for the next two weeks, at astronomical cost, no doubt. Celino scheduled an inspection of the new development to the south. That meant a flurry of meetings and formal dinner engagements, which, if the new Celino was anything like his younger self, he would loathe with great passion. He was both too active and too smart. Time may have taught him patience with less agile minds, but it could hardly teach him how to escape boredom in their presence.

She had reviewed his recent development projects. Celino built beautiful places, full of sunlight and flowers, all of the modern technology seamlessly married with the provincial earthiness. Meli smiled. One could remove a man from the provinces, but one couldn't take the provinces out of the man. He would strive to escape tedium of formality, which meant he would likely stay in his villa on the Terraces and lunch below, among the cafes.

Revenge was sometimes best served hot.

CELINO STRODE down the tiled curve of the Red Terrace. Built into the side of a towering cliff, now honeycombed with metal and plastic-sheathed tunnels, the Terraces consisted of seven platforms, layered one under another, each about a mile long and two hundred yards at their widest. The platforms jutted in gentle curves from the former cliff, housing small shops and eateries. The bottom terrace sat roughly three thousand feet above the plain, while the Red Terrace, where he stood, was situated three levels above it. He wasn't sure about the exact altitude, but the view was magnificent.

The residents of New Delphi were used to heights, but even Celino, as he stopped by the faux wooden rail, was momentarily overcome by the enormity of the landscape. Far below him a vast plain rolled into the distance and beyond it blue cliffs rose, made ethereal by the ocean of air.

Celino resumed his walk, aware of Marcus following like an unobtrusive shadow a few feet behind. Two of his men, Romuld and Ven, stalked behind Marcus.

The breeze brought a whiff of a shockingly familiar aroma. He stopped. He smelled crisp dough with a slight buttery taste and a tantalizing scent of roasted passion raspberry, the only variety of the old planet berry that grew in the southern provinces. The aroma swirled about him and instantly he was five years old, stealing the still warm cone of pastry from the dish and eating quietly under the table, thrilled at his own sneakiness.

"What is it?" Marcus asked softly.

"Passion cones." Celino accelerated, heading toward the source of the scent, until he reached a small cafe with a red overhang. A sign proclaimed A Taste of Dahlia. He rarely entered unfamiliar places. Why risk an ambush?

Celino glanced past Marcus at Ven. "An order of passion cones."

The bodyguard ducked into the shop.

Celino shrugged. Funny how the memory played tricks. He could practically taste the pastry from the scent alone.

Ven emerged from the cafe. Empty handed.

Celino stared.

"The owner says the cones aren't his to sell," Ven said. "I told him to name the price, but he refused."

Celino growled. He wanted the damn cones. He strode into the shop.

The cafe was small, barely more than a counter and six tables. The floor was faux wood, the furnishings vintage Dahlia: sturdy old furniture that would last another century. Only two of the tables were occupied. The patrons watched him like terrified rabbits.

Behind him Romuld activated the scanner that sat over his left eye. A sheet of green light swept over the tables and people sitting at them. Romuld said nothing. The place was clean.

An older man hurried to Celino's side, nervously wiping his hands with a towel. "Sir?"

"Passion cones," Celino said.

The older man twisted the towel in his hands. "You see, the

business is a bit slow. It's a weekday and off-season."

Celino frowned.

The man stammered. "There is a woman. She rents one of my stoves once in a while, because I have the old iron ovens. The old province kind. She pays well. She was the one who made the passion cones. So I can't sell them. I've asked."

The trip down memory lane suddenly became a challenge. "Then I will ask her myself."

The man nodded and pointed to the back. "Through that door, sir."

Celino crossed the floor and ducked through the low doorway. A spacious kitchen stretched before him, filled with the tantalizing aroma of freshly baked dough.

A woman sat at a large table, in a pool of golden light streaming from the window. She wore a sundress the color of burgundy. Her hair was gathered into a thick dark braid that glinted with copper in the sunlight. In her hands was an electronic reader.

She looked up at him, her dark eyes like two bottomless pools on a face tanned to golden perfection. Celino stared.

The woman blinked against the green sweep of Romuld's scanner and raised her eyebrows.

"I'm told you made the cones," Celino said.

"Technically, I'm still making them." Her voice was sensuous and confident, and completely unimpressed with his surliness. She checked her reader's clock. "Thirty seconds left."

"I'd like to purchase them."

"Are you a Dahlian?"

"I don't see how that can be of any consequence."

She rose. She was shorter than he, maybe five four. The thin dress hugged her chest, outlining large, full breasts and a narrow waist. The wide cut of the skirt hid her hips, but judging by the rest of her, her butt was round and plump. She grasped a heat-resistant towel, forced open the stove door and pulled a tray of cones into the light. They looked perfect, golden crispy brown.

"If you were a Dahlian, then you would know that passion cones must be baked with love and given freely. Mothers make them for their children, wives make them for their husbands, and young girls bake them for their lovers. It's bad luck to sell them."

She set the tray atop a stone block and used the tongs to transfer the cones to a small cloth-lined basket. He liked the way she moved, easy, graceful, gliding.

"That's an old superstition."

"Superstitions add texture to life."

She picked up the basket and brought it to the table, and once again he stared, mesmerized by her curves and her bottomless eyes.

"How much?" he asked, and wasn't sure if he was asking how much she wanted for the cones or how much she would charge to let him have a go at her ripe body.

"Not for sale." A little sly light danced in her dark eyes.

Cones or you, he wondered. Her eyes told him the answer: both.

He changed his tactics. "By the same tradition, it's bad luck to turn away a guest from your table. Especially one who arrives in the middle of the meal."

She laughed softly. "So you're from Dahlia after all. I'll make you a deal. I will share my cones. But I have no pink wine to go with them. If you…"

He simply jerked his hand and the sound of rapidly retreating steps announced Ven's departure.

"A bit imperious of you," she said, amused.

He pulled out a chair and sat at the table opposite her. "It'll save us time." He glanced at her reader. A Chronicle of the Reign of Charles IX. "Prosper Mérimée?"

"Indeed."

He didn't think anyone except him read the long forgotten old planet author. "Stories of a more savage time. When men were men and women were…"

"Hauntingly beautiful bronze statues of Venus who crushed

them in their sleep?"

Celino frowned. She didn't simply read the novel, she had read the short stories as well.

"I'm afraid I prefer Colomba to Carmen," she said. "So if you want to discuss the opera, you're out of luck."

He viewed opera as a garish and vulgar spectacle.

Ven entered and placed a bottle of Dahlian Pink on the table. He had activated the icer on the side of the bottle and a delicate feathery frost painted the glass.

"We'll need mugs," she murmured. "Ascanio! Can I trouble you for a couple of mugs?"

Mugs. How...provincial. He hid a smile.

The proprietor scurried into the room, deposited two heavy clear mugs onto the table, and escaped.

Celino popped the cork and poured the wine. A lush pink splashed into the mug. She tasted it. Her eyes widened. "Cerise!"

"Indeed."

"Had I known you would pay for the cones with luxury wine, I would've surrendered immediately."

"Surrendered" conjured an image of her naked in the sheets. Surprising. It had been a long time since he reacted that way to a woman. And she wasn't even beautiful. She seemed to have none of the refined elegance he usually sought.

Where did she come from? What was she doing here? Besides baking passion cones.

He pulled his combat knife from the sheath on his belt and offered it to her handle first. "I believe it's customary to share the first cone."

She took the knife without care, gripped it like a hammer, oblivious to the fact that her fingerprints registered on the handle, and chopped a cone in two. Whatever she was, knife artistry wasn't in her talents. She cut like a cook.

She returned his knife and pushed half a cone toward him. "May you prosper."

"And you as well." His mouth automatically shaped the

response to the old greeting.

She bit into her cone. Celino tasted his, waiting for the three-second diagnostic. No alarms blared in his implant. No poison. He bit a piece, savoring it this time. It tasted like heaven. Neither too sour, nor too sweet. Perfection. He ordered passion cones from time to time and the premier bakeries of New Delphi had nothing on this woman.

His teeth caught something solid. "Lemon rind?" he said in disbelief. To the best of his knowledge, only his mother put lemon rind into the cones.

"You found out my secret." Her pink tongue darted out of her mouth to lick a smudge of the filling off her bottom lip. He wondered if her mouth tasted of cones and pink wine.

"Would your men like some?"

"No," he said.

"They're on duty?"

He nodded and attacked the second cone.

He had eaten three before Marcus leaned over to him. The meeting with the land owners started in less than twenty minutes. Barely enough time to reach the conference hall within his hotel.

He didn't want to leave. He wanted to sit with her in the sunny kitchen, drink pink wine, eat cones, and think of her in his bed.

"Ah. You have to run," she guessed.

"Indeed." He rose. "Thank you. The cones were divine."

She handed him the basket. "Take them."

He hesitated.

She rose and pressed the basket into his hands. "You're leaving the wine with me. It's only fair."

Outside the sunshine made him blink. He slipped the knife out and handed it to Romuld. "Find out who she is."

MELI SAT ALONE in the kitchen. She poured herself another mug. The wine was perfect, delicate, its bouquet leaving a symphony of complimenting flavors on her tongue.

A small part of her had hoped Celino would recognize her. But he didn't. That was how little her existence had meant. She was nothing but a forgotten speck in his past life.

Meli drank the wine.

It had started with a veil.

She vividly remembered it. It was a diaphanous indigo veil that hid the bottom part of her face, leaving only her eyes exposed. When her mother had slipped it onto her, adjusting the band to fit under the knot of her hair, Meli could still see her features in the mirror, but her face seemed broken in half. There was the tan half with her eyes and then there was the lower half under the veil that seemed to belong to someone else.

"Why?" she asked.

Mother sat on the bed. "You are betrothed. The veil lets everyone know that you're off-limits."

The enormity of it failed to penetrate. "But I'm only ten."

Mother sighed. "I voted against it. I think it's a critical error in judgment and I think it will come back to haunt us all. But I was outvoted by the family counsel."

Even at ten, Meli knew that family counsel was law.

"Who am I marrying?"

Mother snapped her fingers. The display hidden in the surface of the mirror ignited. "Engagement," her mother said briskly. A file appeared, opened, and an image of Celino Carvanna filled the screen.

"But he's old!"

"Don't be melodramatic. He's only sixteen. In eight years, when you marry him, you will be eighteen and he will be twenty-four. See, the difference is much less pronounced. And when you're twenty-two and he's twenty-eight, you'll barely notice it."

Meli stared at Celino's face. He was handsome. She had seen him a few times at the garden parties. But he didn't know she existed. "But he isn't interested in me in that way."

"Darling, you're ten. Trust me, if I had any inkling that he was interested in you in that way at this point, they'd have to kill me and your father both to go through with this engagement. He is a very young man. Right now woman to Celino means a set of breasts and a plump bottom."

Mother took her hands into hers.

"You're not a woman yet, Meli. But one day you will be. You won't be beautiful, but you will be attractive and men will flock to you. Me, your aunt Nez, your grandmother, we all have that something that makes men turn their heads and do silly things to entice us into their beds. Don't worry, darling. He will notice you one day. You will hit him like a brick."

The veil itched her chin. Meli scratched. "But why do I have to do this?"

"Because our family and the Carvannas have formed an alliance. On our own, we're both too small to be a significant player in New Delphi, but together we can be a force. Our territory will double. We're sharing technologies and manufacturing facilities. And your betrothal to Celino cements it together the way seal foam cements sections of the spacecraft together."

"What if I don't want to?"

Mother gathered her into her arms. They sat together looking at Celino.

"I will have to do it anyway, won't I?"

"Yes."

"What if he won't like me?" Meli said softly.

Mother fell silent. "I have to be honest with you, Meli. He probably won't like you. And it has absolutely nothing to do with you. As I said, he's a very young man. He's just now coming into his own. Before the engagement he could see freedom on the horizon: independence, however small, from the family. His own aerial. His own place. Freedom to find women and choose his destiny. Our family counsels took all of it away from him with this engagement. The world of his possibilities has been narrowed. He's a gifted, independent boy and he will be bitter about this development. That we can't help. And that's why I didn't want this engagement.

I don't want you to be married to a man who will think of you as a burden."

Mother patted her hair. "But not all is lost, sweetheart. We have it in our power to change his perspective. We must get him to see you not as a rock about his neck but as an ally. Someone who will be on his side no matter what. Someone who will understand him, and listen, and be able to converse with him at his level. A sheltered harbor in his life. You already have a lot in common and we have eight years before you have to marry him. That's time enough to become expert on all things Celino."

And so Meli studied. She learned the recipes Celino liked and practiced cooking them until they were perfect. She read the same books he had read and analyzed them, although she didn't always form the same impression of them. He was interested in business and she had received private tutorship from the candidate of sciences of New Delphi Business Academy. She'd learned the significance of implants, the genealogy of both families, and the frequency of random inborn talents within them. She knew which cologne Celino wore, what colors he preferred, what holofilms he was likely to quote. There were times when she resented him, even hated him, but part of her understood it was self defense against the engagement neither of them had wanted, and the other part, the part that grew stronger and stronger over the years, noticed how brilliant he was, how clever and sharp, and ruthless. As he cut down the competition left and right, she grew to admire his ferocity. And the woman in her began to notice how unbearably handsome he was.

He had left the province shortly after their engagement. Before his departure they were brought together and left alone for a few moments on a balcony. He was spectacular in his Carvanna black, and she was a skinny kid with half her face hidden by a veil.

"I'm sorry about this," he said.

"Me too," she mumbled.

"I want you to understand it wasn't my idea. I'm not a pervert."

He walked away from her, leaving her alone on the balcony pondering his words.

He took to New Delphi like a fish to the ocean. Meli received frequent updates of his legendary financial maneuvers. He was a genius. But he had his flaws: impatience, insensitivity, inability to slow down. Meli had catalogued his weaknesses, knowing she would have to compensate for them.

One evening while in the armory she picked up an ene-ribbon wrist brace and discovered she was a melder. Her mind and body had the power to activate and wield an ene-ribbon. It was an exceedingly rare talent. The chances of it occurring in their bloodline were one to two million. She was brought to the melder adept in the city and trained at a great expense to the family. Her father had insisted that this fact be hidden from the Carvannas, and Celino in particular. She imagined he began to suspect that not all was well with his future son-in-law.

By twenty Celino had doubled the Carvannas' liquid capital. She saw him infrequently, for a few moments during his visits to the ancestral home. He avoided her and their interaction was limited to a few brisk exchanges. They could barely manage a conversation. The older she grew, the more she stammered in his presence, seized by a kind of giddy exaltation born from the knowledge that one day he would be hers. Celino was utterly oblivious to her crush. He was never impolite, but she had come to expect no warmth from those visits. None was owed to her.

Meli would change that. She knew she would.

Then in June, almost exactly six years to the day of the engagement, came the crushing news: The Carvannas reneged on their agreement, severing all financial ties with Galdes. The engagement was off. The blood oaths were undone. The Carvannas cut them loose and it was done at Celino's insistence.

It took Meli about a minute to fully digest all of the implications of the disaster and then she sank on the floor, shaken to her very core by despair. It took her almost five hours to work up the courage to go see him. Meli had no future with him, but if she acted now, before he escaped her reach, she could still have a future.

She put her crushed heart aside and donned a black dress. She came alone, unarmed, still wearing her veil, and Carvanna retainers parted to let her pass. A single soldier led her to the pavilion on the hill. A huge blocky building, it served as the training hall for Carvanna kinsmen for over a century. She walked inside alone and stood at the battle line drawn on the floor.

Celino was in the middle of the floor, a knife in his hand. His torso and feet were bare and he wore only the wide dark practice pants. The lights were off. Shutters shielded the windows, permitting only the narrow rays of sunset that made a grate of light and shadow on the floor. He moved through it, silent, quick, strong like a predatory cat. His knife flashed, rending invisible opponents.

She watched him a minute, crossed the battle line, and stepped into his path. He moved toward her, a dervish of spinning kicks and knife strikes. He didn't look capable of stopping, but she knew better and stood her ground until his knife halted an inch from her throat.

He looked at her with cold eyes. "You've wasted your time."

"I came to convince you to marry me."

He sighed, his sweat-slicked chest rising. "I know. It's not your fault. It's not my fault either. But they chained me with this engagement and I can't live my life on a chain. For six years I did nothing but work. I ate, lived, and breathed numbers. I gave up on the pleasant diversions a man of my age should enjoy. I did it because I wanted to be free. A week ago my contribution to the family exceeded profit generated by Galdes."

"So you delivered an ultimatum: your freedom or your absence."

"In essence, yes. I promised them prosperity if they followed my wishes or my excision if they didn't. It's business. I simply outbid your family. I'm worth more to my kin than this alliance."

"I understand your desire for freedom. But please understand my point. By marrying me you would—"

He waved his hand. "Don't you have any dignity? I have worked for half a decade to escape you. Do you really think you can change my mind by begging? If you were beautiful, perhaps I would consider it for a moment. I've seen you without your veil and you can't even offer me that. But even if you were golden, even if you were the most elegant and refined being on the planet, I would push you aside. I value freedom more."

"Celino!" She needed him to listen, damn it.

"A bit of advice—take off that ridiculous rag." He headed out the door. She rushed after him but he had vanished into the night. Her sixteen-year-old heart lay broken on the floor.

She wrote him several letters, both through the feed and, when he deleted those unread, on actual paper. Her pleas had gone unanswered.

Her god rebelled against his worshipper and he had no mercy to spare.

It happened just as she calculated. Although her engagement was technically broken, until Celino married she remained off limits to kinsmen. First, she had been groomed for another man. Second, Celino might change his mind and decide to marry her and no kinsman wanted to offend New Delphi's newest financial shark. Had her family enjoyed greater influence, she could've found a husband, but none of the smaller families dared to take a chance, knowing the Galdes clan lacked resources to shield them from Celino's wrath. By twenty, having watched an endless stream of leggy blondes pass in and out of Celino's public life, Meli realized that Celino would never marry. He enjoyed his freedom too much. He had turned her into an old maid.

Meli refused to remain a liability. After all, she was a melder. She channeled her frustration into the lethal kiss of the ene-ribbon. After her mother's death, she excised herself from the family, developing a separate life so she could be their silent blade. Over a decade she had killed many to protect her family, always in self-defense and always after a careful study. She had two liaisons, but they were brief and failed to repair her.

Meanwhile, Celino outgrew godhood and became a titan. The Carvannas prospered and grew under his leadership, while the Galdes stagnated.

Now they wanted her to assassinate the man who had doomed her. A man she knew intimately well.

A man whose eyes made her heart skip a beat, despite his unintended cruelty, despite the years, despite the gulf between them and her deep, logical desire to feel nothing for him.

Meli rose. The next few days would prove infinitely fascinating.

CELINO AWOKE EARLY. He lay in bed, staring at the ceiling above him. Around him the bedroom was luxuriously silent.

He dreamt of the woman in the red dress. He dreamt of her ripe golden body in his bed and of dripping honey onto her plump nipples and then slowly licking it off while she laughed. He awoke hard like a rock.

It was a ridiculous adolescent fantasy.

"Romuld. Audio only."

The huge screen on the wall ignited with pale blue. "Sir?" Romuld said softly.

"The woman?"

"The lab lifted two partials from the knife. No match in the aerial database."

So either she didn't own a vehicle, or it wasn't registered.

"The scan showed no implants or Class C or above modifications."

She wasn't a fighter. He already knew that.

"The owner of the shop reported that she stops by occasionally, never more often than twice a month, rents a stove, and bakes pastries. He says it's highly unlikely she will return within the next week or two."

"What did she bake the last time?"

"Apple pie."

Celino cut off the transmission.

And so she breezed into his life and slipped away again. Perhaps she thought she would never see him again. She was wrong. He wanted her and when he wanted something, he always got it.

A woman like her, a lovely, earthy, provincial woman like her, where would she go in New Delphi?

"Naria. Audio only."

A moment passed and then his sister's voice filled the room. "Celino?"

"Where do you shop when you come to the city?"

"Well, good morning to you too!" A child's laughter rang through the transmission. "Where do I shop? Let's see..."

He patiently listened to the long list of children's clothing stores and designer boutiques. Wrong Carvanna. "What about Aunt Rene?"

"Rynok Market. She loves that place."

"Thank you."

He ended the transmission and called up Romuld. "Rynok Market. Find the woman."

THE PRESENTATION of the site manager dragged on. Celino had caught the gist of it within the first five minutes—the site fell behind schedule and it was the fault of the crew, the supplier, the weather, and cosmic gods. The site manager was completely innocent of any wrongdoing and bore no responsibility for anything whatsoever. Celino intended to fire him after his speech, but he permitted the man to state his case.

The display of his personal unit ignited. Romuld's face came into view and his voice spoke into Celino's ear through the audio link. "She's here."

The image blurred and shifted into an aerial view of the market. Romuld had launched a sweeper unit. It hovered above the crowd, unnoticed, its camera sweeping the faces of patrons. The camera zoomed in and Celino saw her. She wore a green dress with a red skirt. It made her look like an upside-down flower. Her hair was down, a windblown mess of dark happy brown. Her face wore a deadly serious expression as she bargained for a bunch of herbs with a vendor. The vendor threw his hands up in exasperation. She raised her eyes to the sky. The vendor shook his head. An ancient ritual of haggling proceeded merrily along, both parties having entirely too much fun for their own good, until finally she walked away from the booth, her bundle of herbs deposited into a small expandable satchel.

"Stay on her," Celino murmured silently, his voice fed into Romuld's audio piece by his implant. "I want to know where she lives."

"Should I tag her?"

"No. Just follow."

The meeting came to its inevitable conclusion ten minutes later. By the time Celino resolved the issue and ascended to the dock housing his aerial, Romuld had sent him her address. She lived only a few minutes from the market, in Old Town.

She owned an old house, pre-second expansion. It perched behind an impact-proof plastor fence disguised as a wall of rocks. As he flew over it and circled the house, he saw the backyard. Filled with bright color, it suggested a garden. He had expected her to have a garden.

Celino landed on the small parking space, noting that no fresh scuffs marked the slab—she didn't own an aerial—and made his way to the door. For a moment he considered knocking, then shrugged, and attached the small disk of the lock breaker to the plate above the electronic lock. The lock breaker's display flashed a couple of times, but remained red. No dice.

Celino tried the door. Unlocked. Utterly ridiculous.

He let himself in.

A small house lay before him. A typical rectangular front hallway. He saw her shoes sitting in a neat row. Straight ahead the hallway ran into the kitchen. He heard a female voice humming and rhythmic strikes of the knife against the cutting board.

On his left the hallway opened into the living space, a large square room, proof of the house being built during the time when people still prized hard copy recordings and pseudo-paper books and needed ample space to store them. The room was mostly empty now and furnished in cool blue. Two soft chairs, a pile of floor cushions in the corner opposite a modestly sized screen on the wall. And at the far wall a sliding plasti-glass door stood wide open, only a thin mesh separating the house from the garden.

Celino strode into the kitchen. He could've sworn he made no sound, but she raised her head. Dark eyes glanced at him and he stopped, arrested by their unexpected beauty. Velvet, brown like the finest coffee, lit from within by her vitality and intellect, those eyes simmered the blood in his veins. With a single look she had awakened a feral need smoldering beneath the surface. He went hard. He would have this woman. She just didn't know it yet.

"What are you doing in my house?" She seemed neither afraid, nor disturbed, rather slightly indignant that he dared to enter without permission.

"You never told me your name." He forced himself to move and sat leisurely in the chair opposite her. The kitchen smelled of subtly spiced stock. A mess of minced herbs lay on the cutting board before her.

"I suppose I best call city security to throw you out."

"Do you think they can?" Not likely. A squad of elite "busters" wouldn't be able to remove him from her presence.

She surveyed the breadth of his shoulders. "Perhaps. You're rather dark and menacing. Are you enhanced enough to support this promise of violence?"

"Yes."

"I see."

She lifted the lid off the pot, releasing a cloud of aromatic flavor into the kitchen, and scraped the herbs into the soup. "What is it you want?"

"You."

"Why?"

He frowned. "I'm not sure. But I'm plagued by dreams involving your breasts and honey."

Her eyebrows crept up. He caught a hint of blush on the tan smoothness of her cheeks and found it at once elating and erotic.

"It's quite adolescent of me, I know," he said.

"You break into the house of a complete stranger, force yourself into her kitchen, and suggest that she should surrender her breasts to you so you can satisfy your honey-dripping fetish. What woman could pass on that invitation?"

"You haven't had many lovers, have you?" He watched her blush fade. It suddenly seemed important.

She blushed again and he smiled, satisfied in her answer. She pointed at the front door with an oversized spoon. "Out."

"What will it take? What should I do to have you?"

"I think you might be a raving lunatic."

He smiled. "But you aren't afraid of me."

She sat in her chair. "No. You don't strike me as a man who would rape."

"Despite me being dark and menacing."

"You like to win." She took a sip from her glass. "And forcing yourself on me would mean you failed in your conquest."

In two sentences she deftly dissected his soul. "I'm Celino Carvanna. Name your dream and I'll make it happen. And then, if you're so inclined, perhaps you could fulfill mine."

"A rather melodramatic declaration, don't you think?" She smiled. Her mouth was soft, her lips pink like the sweet wine they drank.

"Women usually respond well to drama and decisive declarations of lust."

"I'm not that sort of woman. Unfortunately for you, I'm not for sale." She leaned her elbows on the table and rested her chin in her hands. "So far you failed to terrify me and failed to buy me. I'm terribly curious what path you will attempt next."

In his mind he lunged across the table and crushed her mouth with his. "Perhaps I will praise your cooking."

"Ah. Flattery. A bit predictable, but it often works."

"Do you find me attractive?"

She looked him over. Her gaze touched his chest, hidden by black doublet, slid up to caress his shoulders, then his thick neck, lingered on his cheekbones and finally rose to meet his stare. Her eyes were liquid chocolate and he felt a thrilling tension run through him.

"Yes," she said, slightly surprised. "I do."

"Will you let me kiss you?"

"Probably not. But I will share my soup with you, since you're in my kitchen and I'm starved. You seem to be comfortable with rudeness, but I can't let go of my manners and eat in front of you while you stare at me with your iceberg eyes."

"Iceberg eyes?"

"Glacial. The bowls are behind you."

Celino rose. The wall was dotted with standard hidden shelf covers. He tapped the closest one. A shelf slid out of the wall, offering a row of neatly placed bowls. He plucked two and pushed the shelf back into the wall.

She ladled the soup into the bowls. "Would you like to eat in the garden?"

She led him through the house into the garden. Flowers greeted him in every shade and shape imaginable. Dahlias. In his youth, he had spent countless evenings on the balcony of Carvanna house, sitting in a chair, puzzling over a financial riddle, and when he would look up to clear his head, the riot of dahlias blooming in the garden greeted him just like this.

"Take a chair," she offered.

He sat and drank his soup from the bowl. It was delicious, spicy and tart, with an undercurrent of fiery peppers that nipped on his tongue.

They sat together, saying nothing even when they both finished their meal. A feeling of profound calm descended upon Celino. He let the peculiar refreshing serenity sweep through him, bringing him a deeply rooted happiness at simply being alive.

The audio piece piped into his ear for the third time. He was catastrophically late. He rose, bowed to her, and left without a word.

AND THERE IT WAS, Meli reflected. He found her. Less than twenty-four hours. She expected nothing less from Celino Carvanna.

He fantasized about dripping honey on her breasts. A small, satisfied smile curved her lips. It took almost eighteen years, from the skinny ten-year-old girl to the twenty-eight-year-old woman, but Mother proved right. She hit him like a brick.

And she managed to hide that a single glance from him made her entire body hum like a tightly wound string under the hand of a virtuoso guitar player. Celino Carvanna was honeyed poison in her wine. The same delicious fear she had experienced in his presence as an adolescent returned full force, only she was no longer an inexperienced child. She used this fear now, turning it into seductive tension, letting him sense just enough to spur him into open pursuit. Celino was a predator and every predator responded to prey who seemed to run. And when she finally let him catch her, their battle would drive him out of his mind.

She supposed she should be ashamed for still wanting him. Her father would certainly be ashamed if he knew. But her mother would not.

Love was a rebellious emotion, Meli decided. It defied constraints of reason. She no longer cared about the twenty-two year old who, in his rush to freedom, trampled her. She discarded him long ago, except as fuel for revenge. His temple lay in ruin, his statue shattered, his hymnals burned. She would never again worship him or any other.

But the man he had become stirred a deep longing in her. He was darkness. His eyes were ice. He didn't walk, he prowled, confident, powerful, dangerous. He had learned patience and achieved his dreams. And yet, hidden beneath the layers of menace and terrifying competence he remained deeply alone. Just like she did.

He was seductive and it was beyond her not to respond.

A small calculating part of her was glad of it. Celino would sense any insincerity. Luckily for her, when she finally kissed him, she would be perfectly honest in her want. There would be nothing false in her, not in the way she would shiver under the touch of his hands, not in the way she would part her legs for him, letting him drive himself inside her. She would revel in him, drink him in, and every moment of her pleasure would be genuine.

And when he belonged to her, she would finally repay a decade worth of pain in a single brutal dose of reality.

Meli smiled.

CELINO LASTED TWO DAYS.

Shrouded in the comfortable gloom of the evening, her reader on the pillow before her, Meli sensed him at her doorstep before his hand touched the handle and shivered in anticipation. "Lamp," she whispered and a small light ignited in the corner, diluting twilight with soft yellow glow.

A moment later he pushed her door open and loomed in the doorway, a shadow woven of night.

"Don't you ever lock your door?"

"If I did, how would you get in?"

She had no idea how fast he could move. Before the door had a chance to swing shut, slapped by his powerful hand, he knelt before her in the pile of her floor pillows. She raised her hand and drew her fingertips down his cheek. The warmth of his skin sent a tingling pulse into her hand. It fanned the hungry fire in the depth of her. Her insides tightened. She imagined him claiming her, sliding into her, hard and hot, and she kissed him.

The taste of his mouth intoxicated her. He sealed her lips with his. His tongue slid into her mouth, stroking hers in the liquid rapid rhythm. The fire within her burst into an inferno. Her head swam. He released her, and she slid her arms about his neck, molding herself against his iron chest. "Just like that," she whispered into his ear. "Take me just like that."

She licked the corner of his jaw and saw that the ice in his eyes had melted into radiant hungry heat. His hands grasped her tunic and effortlessly ripped the tear-proof fabric. Her soft breasts swung free. She rose to her knees and arched herself against him. His mouth trailed a path of heat from her neck, over her clavicle and down. His hand cupped her right breast, stroking it, squeezing, guiding her erect swollen nipple up. His mouth closed over it. He licked her, painting searing heat across her nipple. She dug her fingers into his back. "More. More."

He licked her again and she purred for him. She was wet and hot and pliant, dying a little with each stroke of his tongue. His hands slid down her back inside her light pants and the thin shimmer of her underwear to cup her butt. He squeezed her and pushed her back gently onto the pillows. She fell for him.

Celino growled like a hungry animal and pulled her clothes off her. She lay before him, in the cushions, her chest rising, her thighs spread. He stared, as if unable to believe that all of her was his.

She lifted herself up enough to grasp his black shirt. "Off," she breathed. "Every last thread."

He pulled off his shirt. His chest was carved by a savage sculptor, each line hardened to perfection by years of martial practice. His skin was bare of hair and in the soft light his torso was golden like a block of amber, and just as amber, when she drew her hand across it, it sent a spark through her. She kissed the shield of ridged muscles on his stomach, reached for his trousers, unfastened them, and slid her hand inside, down the hard shaft of his erection. He growled, thrusting, and she dipped her head and drew her tongue across the top of him, sucking gently.

Celino jerked back from her, shedding his boots and pulling off his trousers in a violent frenzy. She laughed happily, thrilled that he wanted her, and then he grasped her, still laughing, knocked her back onto the pillows, pinning her down with his weight, and kissed her on the mouth, turning her laughter into a low throaty moan. She locked her hands on his muscular back, feeling every inch of his enormous body pressed against her, rigid with need. He kissed her again and again, on the mouth, on the neck, caressing her until everything faded except him. She wanted him, needed him, and yet he teased her with his mouth and his hands, until she could stand it no longer. Finally his iron thigh edged her legs open. He clasped her hands with his and thrust inside, into her moist heat.

A jolt of nearly unbearable pleasure ripped through her. She gasped, but he gave her no time to come to terms with it. He thrust into her again and again, deep, smooth, hard, each push propelling her higher and higher until at last she burst with pleasure. She laughed, unable to contain rapture, opened her eyes, and saw him come with her first squeeze, his eyes filled with ecstasy of her climax and his release.

He eased himself from her and she curled next to him, her head on his chest. His arm trailed down her back and pushed her closer to him. For a long time they lay intertwined and she listened to his heartbeat until she finally fell asleep.

She awoke in the night because he wanted her again. And then again. Some time in the early hours of the morning she called him a savage, but he laughed and seduced her once more with ridiculous ease.

In the morning he discovered he was late, but he stayed for breakfast. Meli served him shockingly sweet coffee in tiny cups, with a side of red arna berries still on the vine and spicy sweet bread.

He barely touched any of it. His grey eyes looked at her with warmth. He took her hand into his and kissed it.

His tenderness caught her unprepared. She was prepared for a brisk dismissal, but he didn't seem to want to let her go. In making her strategy, she never counted on his affection or on the stirrings of absurd pleasure that affection made her feel.

"You're making me feel self-conscious," Meli said. "Did I finally cook something you hate?"

"Come with me."

Meli shook her head. "I have my world. You have yours."

A shadow of former hardness iced over his eyes. "Am I dismissed then?"

She kissed him on the lips, surprising herself with her tenderness. "I wouldn't do well in your ivory financial tower. I will wait for you here instead. Come to me tonight."

He pulled her in his lap. "I could persuade you to come with me."

She smiled. "Ah, the power of sex. Perhaps you could. But why would you, knowing I don't want to go?"

"So I can have you to myself."

"You can have me anyway. Tonight."

He kissed her neck and she shivered.

"Promise me you will lock your door while I'm gone."

"I promise." She whispered the combination into his ear.

"At least tell me your name."

"Meli."

CELINO KNEW someone had entered his aerial the moment he closed the front door of Meli's house. He waited until the vehicle's door slid open and Marcus's pale features greeted him.

"I came close to sending out a search party, my lord," the Anglican said softly when Celino slid into the driver seat.

"You would have rescued me from one of the best nights of my life and then I would have had to kill you. I'm a savage, you know." He guided the aerial straight up, eased it into the flow of traffic and let the autopilot take over. "What have you found out?"

"A lot and nothing. The house is registered to Meli Asole Grey."

"It's a false name," Celino said. Asole and Grey were two characters from Scarlet Sails by Alexander Green. It was a ridiculously obscure old planet book. The only reason anyone would know of it would be by studying the works of the Seventh Romantic Revivalists, who considered Scarlet Sails the purest expression of romanticism. He recalled suffering through Seventh Romantic Revival somewhere between twelve and thirteen. He deeply hated it. "She has an excellent education."

Marcus nodded. "A trace of the name produced nothing. She simply appeared out of thin air about eight years ago. She doesn't own an aerial. She has no health card. Her bank balance is modest, never over three thousand a month. She receives regular deposits from a closed fund held at Colonial Bank. The account is rated B. Hacking their security grid to see who put it there will be long, dangerous, and expensive."

"Do it. Does she own the house?"

"No. It's owned by Colonial. She makes standard rate payments."

"Buy it. Do it through Fontaine, Inc."

Marcus hesitated. "Most likely, she is kin. She is either on the run and doesn't want to be found or she has excised herself from her family."

Celino frowned. The excision was rare. An excised kinsman severed all ties with their family, sometimes of his own free will, sometimes because his family judged him to be harmful to their wellbeing. An excise lost all claim to his inheritance, family profits, and protection. It was a drastic step, never taken lightly. He had threatened excision years ago to free himself and assert his dominion over the family, and he had given the matter a great deal of thought before taking the plunge.

Meli was a mystery. An enchanting mystery. He had never before had a woman who laughed in joy when he brought her to an orgasm. He wanted to do it again.

Occasionally excision was done to provide the family with deniability. Great thieves and assassins had been excised, so they could act as a shadowy arm of their families. The family reaped the rewards, while the excises alone shouldered all of the consequences. He considered that possibility, turning it over in his mind.

She could've killed him last night. He'd gone to her confident in his ability to defend himself, but he hadn't counted on how absorbing she could be. She occupied his attention completely. He had fallen asleep holding her. He slept well too, what little of it he had done last night.

It was highly unlikely that an assassin would possess none of the enhancements customary to her profession.

"Keep digging," he said. He would do some research himself. Tonight.

Celino spent the next night with her. And the next.

On the third morning he surrendered to his fate and cleared his schedule for the rest of the week. He hadn't taken a vacation in five years.

They spent a lazy day together. He snooped through her reader. He thought she had excellent taste until, predictably, he found Scarlet Sails.

"It's an abominable book," he told her.

She smiled. "I like it."

He opened his mouth to argue but she put her fingers on his lips. "I don't require you to like it. Only to accept that I'm different from you."

Later, after they made love in her bed, and she lay next to him, her head resting on his biceps, she said, "Tell me about your lovers."

"They were many and unremarkable," he said. "None of them were like you."

"How am I different?"

"If I lie, will you know?"

"Yes."

"Perhaps that's your answer."

Her knuckles punched his ribs and he laughed.

"Cheater."

"Men don't speak of things like this."

She turned on her elbow and put her head on his chest. "Tell me."

"You set me on fire," he told her. "While you poured me that soup in the kitchen, I had to fight not to lunge across the table and kiss your mouth. But I've felt that way before, sometimes with women who were merely passing acquaintances. I feel comfortable with you. I know it sounds pedestrian, yet it makes you priceless to me. Being with you is effortless."

"Is that so?" she asked softly.

"You're so like me. Sharp, smart, and practical. And so unlike me. I'm a cold ruthless bastard and you are warm and happy. And soft." He trailed his hands down the curve of her breast. "And lovely." He teased her nipple. "Enchanting. Alluring..."

"You don't say..."

He kissed her and whispered into her ear. "And all mine."

"Not all," she told him and left the bed.

"What of your lovers?" he asked her later when they sat in the garden sipping pink wine he had brought. "How many did you have before me?"

"I've had a few."

"Too many."

"How do you know?"

"More than zero is too many."

She laughed.

"Tell me about them."

"There were two. The first was a much older man. I was twenty-one and he was almost forty. I had chosen him very carefully. He was very kind and he was going off planet in a few days. I wanted my first time to be special and worry free."

"Was it?"

"It was pleasant. He was skilled, but I was self-conscious and we lacked passion."

"What about the other man?"

"He was a wanted criminal. I thought he was a dashing rogue." She sipped her wine. "We were together for almost a year. You know a part of me. He also knew a part of me, the part I no longer want to be."

A sharp spike of jealousy pierced Celino's chest.

"Your eyes are frosting over," she noted.

"What part of you did he know that I don't?"

"The part I will keep to myself for now. You don't need to worry, Celino. The man is dead. He proved himself to be just what I thought he was—a rogue—and his greed got him killed."

She sat there, frowning.

"What's bothering you?" he asked.

"You." She glanced at him. "You make me feel happy. I like being with you."

"Why does that worry you?"

"I'm afraid I might disappear."

"I don't understand."

"You will." She nodded. "One day."

He would uncover all her secrets, sooner or later, he promised himself. He only needed patience and time.

They made love in every corner of the house. They spoke of books and ate the food she made. She surprised him with a keen understanding of finances and he amazed her with his knowledge of dahlias. He secretly ordered a necklace of blood onyx that cost more than the latest luxury aerial. He had it delivered to the house, but she refused to take it. He cooked for her instead and she was delighted.

He had never met a woman so rich, in her warmth, in her mind, in her vitality. And she had given all of herself to him. He felt blessed.

His bliss lasted for three days. On the fourth, the terra plant in Ogavia exploded.

MELI STOOD BEFORE THE SCREEN.

"I will be back in twenty-four hours," he had said. "Wait for me. Please."

She could still feel his good-bye on her lips.

This was it. This was her chance and she wouldn't get another. Her instincts told her that once he returned, he would mount a full assault to bring her into his life completely and she was no longer sure she could resist. She was in love with Celino Carvanna.

She had to bring it to the brutal conclusion now or forever give up on her revenge. She had promised herself at the start of the mission that she would remain strong and finish it, but she'd grossly underestimated her own heart.

It would be so easy to surrender. To simply let him carry her off, to become his. He would never have to know the truth.

Twelve years, she reminded herself. Twelve years of rejection and quiet pain, of feeling broken, as if a vital part of her was lost. Twelve years of controlled anger.

A storm was locked inside her and it was tearing her apart.

She cried and when her sobs exhausted her, she washed her face and once again faced the screen.

You can't smelt happiness from a lie. She knew him, but he did not know her.

She had to end it.

CELINO WAS ENRAGED. The first time Meli had ignored his call, he dismissed it. Perhaps she was in the shower or out at the market. He was in the middle of a smoking ruin awaiting excavation of the reactor and his time was limited to a few precious seconds.

The second time she refused to accept him, he called the man he had left watching her house. The man's personal unit was set to Do Not Disturb.

Worry shot through him. Ignoring the explanation of the diagnostic engineers, he stole a minute of precious time to queue up the camera he had planted in the garden on his personal unit. The camera captured the door and he saw Meli move past the screen inside. He pinged her again and watched her ignoring his call.

Perhaps his man was inside. Perhaps she had invited him in. Maybe he was in her bed.

His face must've turned dark because people around him fell silent. He moved and they scurried out of his way, reading death in his eyes.

An hour later, when he ended the investigation and entered his aerial, he saw a notification of a private message. He locked the doors and brought it up. A "recording disabled" warning popped up—the message would play only once. He wouldn't get a chance to keep it or replay it. "Accept," he ground out through his teeth.

Meli filled the screen. Her hair was pulled back. She wore a grey tactical vest over a grey shirt. He had no idea she owned one.

"Your man is in the kitchen. I tranquilized him, but he should come to his senses by the time your crew gets here. I'm leaving you, Celino."

Pain lanced him.

"This is the end. You will never see me again. A man once told me that even if he met the most elegant and refined being on the planet, he would push her aside, because he valued his freedom more. This is me pushing you aside, Celino. After years of waiting, I'm finally free of you."

He forced himself to punch through the pain clawing at him and concentrate on her words. They seemed hauntingly familiar but he couldn't recall if he had said them or if they were said to him. He knew he had heard those words spoken before.

"Thank you for my freedom. I will strive to never think of you again. Farewell."

The screen went dark. He felt oddly calm. Empty. Cold. He sat before the dark screen, patiently waiting to feel something. Anything at all.

Finally a spark of emotion flared in him. He puzzled over it and recognized what it was. Hot, blinding rage.

It took him less than an hour to cover the distance that typically demanded two and a half. He nearly burned out the aerial's engine. When he dropped out of the sky at reckless speed to land on the slab before her house and stepped out of the cabin, his crew recognized signs of danger and gave him a wide berth. Only Marcus dared to approach him. Celino looked at his face. The Anglican shook his blond head. Meli had escaped.

Inside, the house was gutted. The linen, the pillows, every scrap or fabric or cloth was gone. Her terminal was missing, removed from the wall. The kitchen lay barren, every item sanitized.

Celino found the biotech. "Tell me you have something."

The woman shook her head. "The place is sterilized. She did a complete sweep, probably using a bioscanner. There are no traces of biologicals except for the plants in the garden."

He growled. He'd had countless opportunities to obtain a DNA sample, but he consciously had set them aside, determined to reconstruct her secrets from conversation alone to satisfy his cleverness. Back then, he thought he had all the time in the world.

Now she had obliterated every trace of herself and vanished.

He would find her. He would find out why.

The garden flashed in his head. He had seduced her on the soft grass in the garden three days ago. He remembered sun on her face and her succulent body against the green. She smiled at him from the depth of his memory and he steeled himself against another stab of pain.

Celino strode into the garden and knelt on the patch of grass. Any liquid traces of their coupling had long vanished. He scanned the area, his vision heightened by his fury, and saw a single long hair tangled in the dahlia stems. She'd missed it. The signatures of the plants had dampened her bioscanner and the hair had gone unnoticed.

He untangled it gently, as if it were made of the most precious metal, and took it to the biotech. "Run a match against kinsman database."

He waited next to her while the DNA sequencer purred, comparing the hair to the known families.

"Appalachi, three percent," she reported. "Patel, seven point two. Vinogradov, four percent..."

Garbage, he thought furiously.

"Galdes, seventy-nine point one percent."

He whipped around. The genetic makeup within the families varied to a significant degree. Anything over seventy percent was considered a definitive match.

A terrible suspicion flared in his mind. But he wanted proof.

He spun to Marcus. "I want access to the Galdes files. I don't care how many alarms you set off or what you have to do."

Three hours later he stood behind his best two hackers peering at the triumvirate of data screens. If he could do anything in his current condition, he could inspire fear. They had breached the security of the Galdes files in record time.

Only the top of the family would have access to an excise. "I want all outgoing transmissions from Lyon, Azare and Angel between the tenth and seventeenth." A week's range, extending back from the first time they met.

A long list filled the screens. "Eliminate all known Galdes terminals."

The list shrank to a fifth of its size.

They hit gold an hour into the viewing. When Meli's face filled the screen, he almost didn't register that they had found what he was looking for.

"...a difficult task," Angel said.

Meli's eyes were calm. "No more jobs. I've retired."

"This is a personal request, Meli. From Father."

He watched her close her eyes. She carried on the conversation, waiting for something, standing absolutely still.

A smooth disk of interceptor slid from the hallway behind her. Her eyes remained closed.

The interceptor slid closer, its cannon adjusting to the target.

A translucent green ribbon struck from her, impossibly fast. The interceptor crashed to the floor, smoking.

"Good God," Angel's voice intoned.

"A melder," Marcus hissed. His eyes had gone wide. "I've let you walk into the house of a melder without a guard."

"You couldn't have known."

"I'm…"

"I don't hold you responsible," Celino snarled. "You couldn't have known." He turned back to the screen. "Replay the last ten seconds."

He watched her slice the lethal machine in half. Precise. Elegant. Economical in her movements. She was beautiful.

And yet she didn't kill him. For days he had been at her mercy, but never once did she attempt to attack him. Having watched her in action, he was certain he wouldn't have survived.

Why?

"Retina match to the Galdes personnel files," he said numbly. "Anything with security B or above."

Meli's eyes filled the screen. The computer analyzed the tiny patterns, the personnel files cycled on the left and then a match filled the other half of the front screen. The girl on the screen was much younger. Eighteen at most. Her eyes shone, incandescent with hope. His rage died, frozen into a solid block of ice.

"Identify," he said, barely recognizing his own voice.

"Imelda Anara Galdes. Daughter of Lyon Galdes, sister to…"

"Enough."

Celino closed his eyes, rubbing the bridge of his nose with his fingers. He remembered the source of her words now. He had thrown them in her face twelve years ago.

"There are hidden files attached under her name," one of the hackers said.

He forced himself to look up. "Bring them up."

Two files. Engagement and Excise.

"Leave me."

They filed out of the room, all except Marcus. "Leave me," he repeated. The Anglican bowed and retreated from the room.

Celino sank into a chair.

"Engagement," he said grimly.

A picture of his younger self looked at him. He scrolled past it impatiently. A list of the books from his library, each title with his personal notes. She seemed to have added her own. "Celino: *liked it but the main character lacked discipline*. Meli: *agreed*." Next title. "Celino: *garbage*. DNF. Meli: *tedious beginning but worthwhile finish*." By Scarlet Sails, he had written: "*Pure sap*." She added her own note, *"Celino, you're an idiot."*

A list of holofilms, again annotated with two sets of notes. His school notes, pages and pages and pages of them. She studied him as if he was one of the ancient masters and she a disciplined devotee. She had access to his notes. She must've made a friend among the Carvannas.

He scrolled. A collection of recipes. A recipe for passion cones. A note scribbled with a stylus on the screen marked the corner. *"Don't forget the lemons, Meli!"* He recognized his mother's small script. His own mother had conspired against him.

No wonder he felt at ease with Meli. She knew him, intimately knew him. She'd read his notes and his ramblings and peered into his mind. Why had she done it? He searched his mind and stumbled onto an answer that shook him. She had done it so they would be happy. She had expected to be his wife. She understood he would resent her and so she strove to become more than his burdensome spouse.

He scrolled past years of his school work. His financial machinations. She had analyzed these as well. On Rhomian acquisition she had written, *"Brilliant. Proof that Bavani can stick his Way of Management up his arse."*

Other notes followed, punctuating the records.

"Continues to lack in patience."

"I can't believe he has done this."

"Either he's a financial genius or a ruthless brigand, who simply doesn't care. Perhaps both."

He wanted to read on, fascinated, but he wanted to find her more. "Lyon's schedule, next twenty-four hours."

It was surprisingly easy to capture Lyon Galdes and both of his sons. They didn't expect a brazen assault in full daylight. He had led the crew himself. They took the three men just outside Cantina restaurant. Bound and gagged, the Galdes were stuffed into the armored aerial and whisked away without an incident.

In the air he loosened Angel's gag. "Your sister. Where is she?"

"I don't know," the youngest Galdes snarled. "She was supposed to kill you. Why aren't you dead?"

"That's what I would like to know."

He questioned them all in turn and once he slid open the door and held Angel by his legs upside down above a thousand-foot drop, he became convinced they were telling the truth. They had no idea where Meli had gone.

Celino had them tucked away in his compound. Thirty hours had passed since her transmission. He hadn't slept or eaten and still he had no idea where she was.

He had to think like her. If he were her, where would he go?

It came to him finally. He took a fresh aerial from his garage and headed to Dahlia.

THE OLD TRAINING hall was dimly lit with portable lanterns. Four interceptors hovered, slowly transversing its length. In the center

Meli stood, wearing a light T-shirt and loose pants. Her eyes were shut.

Celino stopped short of the battle line. He didn't know how she had gotten past the guards, but nothing she did any longer surprised him.

She opened her dark eyes and looked at him. The interceptors came within censor range and streaked to her from four sides.

"I never intended to kill you," she said. The translucent green ribbon snapped from her hand with ungodly speed and four dismembered metal husks crashed to the floor. "I wanted you to know what it felt like. Angel's intel is always excellent. The opportunity was too good to pass on it."

"I was cruel," he said. "I still am."

"I know." She walked across the floor to the first interceptor, picked it up and tossed it into a plastic bin. She still had the same gliding smoothness to her movements that drove him wild. He trailed her on the safe side of the battle line.

"Why are you here?" she asked.

"You have my heart. Where would I go without it?"

"Home, Celino."

"Not without what is mine."

She paused and looked at him with her velvet eyes. "I was never yours."

"When I made you climax and laugh, when you fell asleep in my arms, when you smiled at my jokes and reached for me, you were mine."

"What you think of as love are the last splashes of your dying lust. Don't you have any dignity? Do you really—"

"—think you can change my mind by begging?" he finished for her. He crossed the battle line and strode to her, his movement stalking and sleek. He knew every inch of the old gymnasium. He was a predator in a familiar territory. She tensed as he came near and he stopped a few feet away from her. "I didn't come here to beg. You were promised to me and I came to claim you."

She sighed. "I've forgiven you for breaking the engagement a long time ago. I have never forgiven my family or yours for forcing it on us, but I've forgiven you. You were fighting for your freedom. I respect that."

"Then why are you punishing me?"

"Because you wouldn't listen to me, Celino. Had you married me for one day and divorced me the next, I would be free. I would have proof that you no longer wanted me. That's what I had come to ask of you that night. One day. You didn't have to consummate the marriage, you didn't have to attend the wedding, you had only to sign the damn paper and then, twenty-four hours later, sign another. I would've been released. Free to choose a mate, free to make my own future, just like you."

"You were anyway," he said, puzzled.

"Nobody wanted me, Celino!" The ribbon struck from her hand, mincing the closest interceptor into electronic gravel. "They were afraid that one day you might change your mind, show up on their doorstep, and demand restitution for stealing your bride. You didn't even marry. The rest of the kinsmen didn't expect you to lay claim to me, but they couldn't ignore the possibility that you might. Just like you're trying to now."

It finally dawned on him. He bought his freedom with hers.

"I never meant for it to happen."

She faced him. "I hope that you truly love me. I hope it hurts."

"It does. I had no idea it could hurt this much."

She snapped her wrist brace open, sank to the floor, and let her weapon slide from her hand. "Go away, Celino."

"I can't. If I could rip out my heart and give it to you to make you happy, I would. I'm not a good man. I'm a coldblooded, brutal, terrible bastard. But I feel human when you're near me and I know you feel at peace in my presence. Be with me, Meli. I swear I will do everything in my power to make you happy. I will protect you. I will be your sheltered harbor. You will never have to hide from me."

She shook her head in apathy. "You don't even know me."

"I know that you think Magyar's Revenge started slow but

finished well and you consider me a fool for not forcing myself to read past the beginning chapter. I know that you don't lack in patience and that you consistently forget that the constant of standard return on the planet is 4.58, not 4.56. That's why all your calculations differed from mine on the breakdown of Parson Takeover."

It had taken him eight hours to reach Dahlia and he had taken a booster shot to keep himself awake so he could memorize her notes.

She glanced at him. "You hacked the Galdes database. I thought those files were destroyed."

"I did and they aren't. I know the details of every assassination you have ever done. They requested sixteen of you and you did eleven, all of which were retaliations for violence done to your family. I think the risks you took with Garcia were idiotic." He knelt by her. "I also kidnapped your father and your brothers. I would've tortured them if I thought they knew where you were."

She laughed softly, but without humor. "That is an odd way to endear yourself to me."

"I never claimed to be kind or virtuous. But for you, I will be." He swept her into his arms, holding her back against his chest, wrapping her with his body. She jerked away from him, but her advantage lay in precision, not in strength, and he restrained her with laughable ease. "I love you, Meli. I didn't love you when you were sixteen, but I love you now. I'm sorry. I'm sorry I ruined your life. But I will help you build a new one. Be with me."

"Let me go."

He growled his frustration. "You're sentencing us both to misery. In the name of what, Meli? Haven't you been miserable enough? Wouldn't a more fitting punishment be sentencing me to a lifetime of making you happy?"

"Let me go, Celino."

"I can't," he whispered and kissed her hair.

He couldn't force her. He couldn't bind her to himself if she didn't want him. His muscles tensed. He went rigid, fighting against a sharp physical need to hold her, snarled, and finally opened his arms. She rose. "I have lived with this for over a decade. You broke me, Celino. You stole my future and my family treated me like a leper. I had excised myself to escape their pity. You can't fix it with one night of reading through my old thoughts."

He watched her walk away and felt his heart shatter for the second time.

In the morning, Celino Carvanna retired.

CELINO SAT on the second-story wrap-around balcony on a large lounger couch. A reader lay in his hand. A frosted glass of tea rested next to him. Below him dahlias bloomed. Two years had passed, but he still felt a sharp spike of pain when he looked at them. They reminded him of her. He forced himself to glance at them once in a while. Perhaps he had become masochistic, he wondered, raising his gaze.

Meli stood among the flowers.

She wore a simple sundress of vivid red. She had cut her hair. Short and layered, it framed her face in a light cloud.

She had bypassed his guards. It didn't surprise him.

Meli crossed to the house and took the stairs up to the balcony. When she finally sat in a chair next to him, tucking her feet under her, and he caught a slight scent of citrus from her hair, he decided she was real.

"I should've never let them do it to me," she said. "Even at ten, I should have known better. I should've never dedicated myself to becoming an accessory to you."

"You did what any child would have done. Your parents suggested it, encouraged it, and praised you when you excelled at it. The responsibility is theirs and mine. Unfortunately, I turned out to be a self-absorbed arrogant asshole," he said. "Both times."

"The Carvanna finances are suffering. They are threatening to excise you, because you refuse to rescue them from themselves."

He wondered how she had found out that bit of highly guarded information. "They also demand that I turn over my personal funds to the family to bail them out. They won't excise me. They're too attached to the possibility that I might change my mind and return from retirement."

She arched her eyebrows. "Will you?"

He shook his head. "'I've lost the taste for it."

"You lie. I've read the INSA file."

He grimaced. "It takes a special kind of worm to attempt a hostile takeover of a hospital network run by a charity. Even at my worst, I wasn't that heartless. It was a one-time pro-bono rescue."

A little light danced in her eyes. "And Vinderra Wineries?"

"They were going under and I've always enjoyed their wine. Alfonso was taken in by an unscrupulous accountant. It was simply a matter of professional pride."

"And the fact that he has six children had absolutely nothing to do with your involvement?"

"Precisely."

"And the Arid Foundation account?"

"It was a pleasant diversion. I was bored."

"Your family is quite serious, you know."

He shrugged. "I couldn't care less."

They sat in silence.

A cynical thought occurred to him. "Did my family pay you to force me from my retirement?"

"No. I doubt I could." She smiled at him, and Celino felt his throat close. "You enjoy being the caped crusader of the financial world entirely too much."

"I've served the family long enough. What I do now is my own affair."

She laughed. "That look was pure Celino. You almost never look like that anymore."

"You've been watching me?"

She nodded and pointed to the east. "I live over there. I bought Nicola's orchard."

He stared at her, incredulous. "How long ago?"

"Six months."

Fury swelled in him. She had been living next to him for half a year and nobody told him about it. Marcus had to have known.

"Why are you here?" he ground out.

"Because I love you," she said. "I did my best to shame myself into denying it, but I can't. I ran half across the planet and then came back so I could live for glimpses of you at the marketplace. I'm so utterly pathetic."

"So why come back now?"

"Because I know how excision feels," she said softly. "I didn't want you to go through it alone."

She moved to rise. He covered the distance between them in a fraction of a blink and swept her off her feet, crushing her to him. The scent of citrus swirled about them, the heat of her body ignited his, and he sealed her mouth with his, hungry for a taste. She threw her arms around him.

"I'm no longer Celino Carvanna," he said, kissing her. All that he was, all the power, respect, prestige that came with being the head of a kinsman family, he had left it all behind.

"And I'm no longer Imelda Galdes," she whispered, her voice a breath in his ear.

"I fly to New Delphi every month to that damn eatery, hoping to see you there. I bought your house and I sit in your garden, like some sort of imbecile, hoping you'll come through the door."

Celino tasted salt and realized she was crying. He swallowed, pressing her tighter to him. A curious feeling claimed him, a powerful lightness. He felt strong, capable, and yet impossibly content. "I love you," he said, his voice a raspy growl. "Promise me you won't vanish this time."

"I promise," she said and kissed him back.

SILVER SHARK

Prologue

In the course of space colonization, there arose a need for humans with enhanced abilities - men and women who could survive harsh conditions, who were superb warriors, gifted hunters, and brilliant scientists.

Some enhancements were technological in nature: an array of implants with various functions. Their effect ended with the death of the person who carried them. Other improvements were biological and these enhanced capabilities persisted, lingering in the bloodline, changing and mutating into new abilities in the offspring of the original carrier. It was quickly realized that the advantage of these biological enhancements lay in their exclusivity. Thus, the biologically enhanced united and shut down all further biological modification.

Collectively known as kinsmen, these exceptional beings gave rise to several dozen families, which now form the financial elite of the colonized planets. The kinsmen strictly control their numbers and their loyalty to their families is absolute. Like the Sicilian mafia families and feuding Corsican clans of the old planet, the kinsmen exist in constant competition with each other. It is this competition that rules the economy, begins and ends wars, and drags human civilization to greater technological and scientific progress.

Kinsmen with the ability to telepathically attack the minds of others are called psychers.

Chapter One

Claire awoke early. Her grey ceiling hung like a bleak shroud above. She looked at it, trying to gather enough willpower to leave the bed.

A digital screen flared into life on the wall, presenting her with a digital clock. A female voice with a flat, computer- generated intonation announced, *"Good morning. You have thirty minutes until scheduled departure to work, Captain Shannon."*

She stared at the ceiling.

"Twenty-nine minutes. You are now one minute behind schedule."

"Twenty-eight minutes. You are now two..."

"Dismissed," Claire said.

The screen died. She sat up and pushed off the bed. Around her, the apartment offered a dreary monochromatic palette: grey walls, dark floor, paler ceiling. No splash of color interrupted the drabness.

She walked to the window. The shutter's photosensor detected her presence, and the thick panels of grey plastic slid aside. She was on the fortieth floor. Buildings rose around her, half-a-kilometer-tall rectangular boxes, separated by deep grim canyons of narrow streets. Above the city, the smog-smothered sky sifted chemical rain. The rainwater wet the sides of the uniform skyscrapers, bleaching long drip-trails in the concrete.

Her quarters were in the barracks of Intelligence Building 214. The apartment where she grew up with her mother was located ten blocks east. Looking out of her window, she could tell no difference between the view from her current rooms and that apartment. Even the bleach patterns seemed the same.

If she were to leave the city, which was practically impossible, she would find a barren rocky plain. The planet of Uley had only two relatively small land masses, neither of them inviting. The Eastern Continent was colonized three hundred and twenty seven years ago by the Melko Corporation. Three years later the Brodwyn Mining Consortium landed on the Western Continent. Melko voiced their claim to the entire planet and demanded that all Brodwyn colonization efforts cease immediately. Brodwyn declined to comply.

Both conglomerates began rapid exploitation of natural resources in an effort to achieve industrial and military superiority. Every industry on either continent was designed to serve the arms race. Forty years before she was born, the hostilities exploded into an open conflict: Melko against Brodwyn, Native against Invader.

She was a Brodwyn retainer, an "evil invader," if the propaganda of the Melko group was to be believed. She could've just as well have been born a "greedy native" on the opposite side of the planet. It would have made absolutely no difference to her life. The war had dragged on for so long, with both sides claiming they were winning and trying to demoralize the other, that whatever personal victories she had achieved seemed completely meaningless.

Claire stared down to the hazy street below. If she opened the window and jumped, she would fall for about ten seconds before splattering on the pavement.

If she jumped.

To end one's own life was the most unnatural urge, but

standing there by the window, she couldn't really muster any anxiety about it. She simply didn't care one way or the other.

"You have fifteen minutes until scheduled departure..."

"Dismissed."

Claire stripped and stepped into the shower. The lukewarm water washed over her. She pushed the knob all the way to HOT, but the water remained mildly warm. Heat, like all other resources, had to be conserved. They were at war.

They had been at war for the last sixty-eight years. War everlasting.

She stepped out of the shower, toweled off her hair, and put on her undergarments and her grey Intelligence uniform with black captain stripes on the left shoulder.

"You have one minute until scheduled departure..."

She stepped into the hallway. The door hissed closed behind her. She took the elevator to the seventh floor, to the mess hall. It was half full, as always, and she scanned it with her mind out of habit. People moved aside for her, an automatic privilege of rank afforded to her captain stripes painted in black. Most had inert minds. A few with a predisposition to psycher activity had thoughts that luminesced slightly, and to the right, at the usual table, four soldiers of her unit glowed. She shut down the mind vision, picked up her tray with a mound of nutrient paste on it, took her vitamin-enriched water, and went to join them.

The psychers stood at attention at her approach.

"At ease."

They sat as she took her usual spot. Nobody smiled. They were at war, after all, and extreme expression of emotion was frowned on, as was bright color, loud noise, and leisure. If they did smile, someone would come up and ask, "Why are you smiling? Don't you know we're at war?"

She didn't examine their minds out of courtesy but she'd learned to read their faces, and she noted the small signs of relaxation: the softening of Nicholas' lips; the way Masha held her spoon, picking at the paste; Dwight's easy pose; Liz's nails, sheathed in transparent coating... manicured nails. Something new.

"Good morning, Captain," Liz murmured. Slight, with thin blond hair cut short, she seemed washed out, her skin nearly transparent, her hair almost colorless.

Claire envied her. Of the five of them, Liz was the youngest, barely seventeen. She still had some impulse, some spark of life. She'd joined the unit last year, and since then keeping her alive during the missions had proven to be a full-time job. It was a job the rest of them shared, but Claire shouldered the lion's share of it.

Liz's brain activity spiked, her thought tentatively brushing against Claire's mind. Claire accepted the communication, opening the link between them.

"I was wondering if I could get a plant," Liz said. *"For my room. I was wondering if you knew where I could get one."*

"It will be confiscated," Claire responded.

"Why?"

"Because a plant requires nutrients, light, and water. It will be tagged as inappropriate expenditure of resources."

The younger woman recoiled.

"I'm sorry," Claire told her aloud.

Liz ducked her head. "Thank you, Captain."

A vague feeling of alarm tugged on Claire. The other psychers sensed it as well and the five of them turned in unison toward the incoming threat.

Major Courtney Rome was making his way through the mess hall toward them. His psych-blocker implant was on, smudging his mind. Smudging but not obscuring. No psych blocker could lock out a psycher of her level completely.

Her team's minds dimmed around her, as her soldiers snapped their mental shields in place. Courtney couldn't read their minds: they simply reacted to a perceived threat on instinct.

Courtney halted a few feet from them. She liked calling him by his first name in her mind. If he ever found out, he would take it as an insult, which it was. Trim and middle-aged, Courtney wore a flat expression. She looked past the blocker into his brain and saw anxiety churning. He came to deliver unpleasant news. He never brought any other kind.

She rose and the rest of her team stood up.

"Captain Shannon, join me for a private consultation."

She followed him to one of the booths lining the wall. They sat. A transparent disruptor wall slid from the slit in the wall, sealing the booth from the rest of the dining hall with a sound-proof translucent barrier.

"Your latest psychological evaluation showed abnormalities." Courtney said. "We are no longer confident that you are giving your all to the war effort."

"Has my performance been lacking?" she asked.

"No. Your performance is exemplary. That's why we're having this conversation."

Claire saw it in his mind: Courtney believed she should be decommissioned, but she was too valuable. Kinsmen like her, with psychic power, came along about one in every six million, and the decision to keep her breathing was made above his pay grade. She could crush his mind like a bug, psych blocker or no.

Claire leaned back, putting one leg over another. "When we're done here," she said, not sure what possessed her to continue speaking, "you will return to your office where you will read reports and push pseudo paper. It's your job. I will go to my job, where I'll have to murder people."

Courtney studied her. "They are the enemy."

"These people I kill, they have children, loved ones, parents. Each of them exists within a network of human emotion. They love, they are loved, they worry. When I sear their minds, all of that ends. They have no choice about engaging in a fight with me, just as I have no choice in being here. For doing this, I am praised and rewarded."

"Your point?"

"There is something wrong with a system that glorifies a person for the killing of other human beings."

"They will kill you if you don't kill them first. They won't hesitate."

She sighed. "What are we fighting for, Major?"

"We're fighting for the control of the planet. The winner will get to keep Uley, of course."

"Have you looked outside, Major? I mean really looked? Keeping Uley isn't a victory; it's a punishment."

Courtney leaned on the table. "I've been doing this a long time, Captain. You are not the first to crack-you won't be the last. Not everyone has the resolve to keep up the fight. But you can be sure that when your time comes, you won't simply be decommissioned. If I were you, I'd keep it together as long as possible, because I am always watching and when you stumble, I will be there."

She had gone too far to care about a threat. "I was taken from my mother when I was fourteen years old," she told him. "She was sick when I left. I wasn't allowed to look after her. The Building Association had to take care of her."

"That's what the Building Associations are for," Courtney said. "They're there to shoulder the responsibility for the residents of the building, so people like us can fight. Everyone must do their part."

"My mother died when I was twenty-two. In those eight years I was permitted to see her three times. There is a child sitting at the psycher table now, Major. She was taken away from her family when she was twelve. It's getting worse. When will it end?"

"When Melko surrenders." He slid a datacard across the table. "Your mission for today, Captain. Penetrate the secure block of the Melko bionet, burn the data, and get out with your minds intact. Brodwyn expended too many resources on your training to lose you."

CLAIRE SHANNON DASHED through the woods. Tall trees thrust to the distant skies on both sides of her. Their dark limbs scratched at each other, their jagged branches thrusting out like talons ready for the kill. Behind her, the team sprinted, single-file. Lean, furry, they surged through the woods on all fours, their clawed paws digging into the forest floor as they ran. She saw them as beasts with glowing eyes. No doubt they saw themselves as something else.

Many years ago the need for faster data processing forced larger corporations and governments to implement biological computer systems that seamlessly integrated with the inorganic computers. It was discovered that only psychers could connect directly to the bionet and that the connection overwhelmed their minds. The human brain couldn't cope with the tremendous influx of information, and it deluded itself by turning code and synthetic neurosignals into a dream, interpreting the streaming data as a familiar environment, knitted from the individual psycher's memories and imagination.

Every psycher perceived the bionet differently. For Nicholas it was hell with molten lava and fire-belching dragons; for Liz it was a mountain pass strewn with snow, where avalanches and snow creatures waited at every turn. Claire saw a forest. Code became trees, secure data turned into fortified castles, and enemy psychers turned into monsters. If it looked scary, it was a threat.

A hint of movement made her spin in mid-step. A large red-eyed bird with wicked dinosaur jaws instead of a beak raised its wings, preparing to dive at her from a tree branch.

Claire leaped.

The bird swooped down, talons out, teeth-studded jaws opened wide. Claire turned her head, throwing her body right. The jaws missed her by a fraction of an inch.

Her silvery fangs closed on the bird's long neck, piercing flesh. The pressure of her jaws crushed the vertebrae, the synthetic neurosignals conjuring the taste of blood in her mouth. They dropped to the ground, the bird flailing under her.

The rest of the team dashed past them.

Claire planted a clawed paw on the bird's head and ripped, tearing the neck in two.

The bird stopped moving.

Threat neutralized. An enemy psycher was dead.

Claire sprinted after the line of beasts, caught up, and sped by them, resuming her place at the head of the pack. She always took the point. She was the strongest psycher and it was her duty as an officer to protect the rest of her team.

The bird's dimming eyes lingered in her memory. She had terminated a human mind. She would have to kill others before the mission ended. She would do it today to keep Liz and the rest alive, but eventually the Intelligence would send her on a solo mission, and she wasn't sure what the outcome of it would be.

Claire scanned her environment. The woods before them were clear. Deserted. Anxiety pulled at her mind. Where were the enemy psychers? She had just killed one - usually that meant a concentrated assault. The branches should be teeming with them.

She twisted to glance back. Only one beast followed her - Nicholas, his coat a pale grey. He took another step and exploded into a hundred tiny dark ribbons, melting into nothing.

The shock punched her.

Claire shot out of the bionet and out of her chair, her vision still a blur. A blink and she saw the room: gun-grey walls, a long console, five chairs by it, one empty - hers, and four others supporting prone bodies, her teammates, her soldiers, each with a gaping hole in the back of the head. In a split second she saw it all: the jagged edges of the head wounds, the red blood dripping on the floor from Liz's blond hair, and Major Courtney Rome, a smoking gun in his fingers, his pale grey Intelligence uniform splattered with crimson spray and brain matter. Courtney's face was slack. His mouth drooped down. His eyes stared at her, hollow.

She grasped his mind in a steel fist, ripping through the feeble protection of the psych blocker like it was tissue paper. He cried out and dropped the gun. She forced his brain to haul him upright, every muscle painfully rigid, his body barely balanced on his toes.

They were dead. This morning all of them had eaten a spare breakfast in the commissary. They shared coffee. Liz hid her new nails. Now they were dead. She had protected them for so long and he'd put a gun to their heads and murdered them one by one.

"Why?" she snarled.

"The war is over," Courtney whispered. "We lost."

"What?"

"We lost," he repeated, his voice a hoarse squeak. "The Headquarters sent out an emergency bulletin five minutes ago. Melko is occupying our continent. The surrender security protocol was initiated. I have to terminate you. You know too much."

She seared his mind. Death was instant. He didn't have the time to scream.

As his lifeless body dropped to the floor, Claire turned and pushed the dimmer switch on the console. The room turned dark. Her fingers flew over the keypad.

The opaque window in the wall before her faded, revealing the interior of the Intelligence compound below. People dashed back and forth across the floor.

She pushed a key, letting the audio feed filter into the room. Gunfire punched the silence. Massive shredders whined, crunching electronics and slicing pseudopaper into atomic dust. Chaos reigned.

The war was over.

Her heart hammered in her chest. Her pulse pounded through her head, too loud in her ears. Claire stared at the four corpses in their chairs. She wanted to hug Liz and cry.

She couldn't give in to panic and shock. She had to think.

She was a Type A Psycher. An imminent threat. If Melko Corporation found her, she would be killed immediately. When you lost a war, you didn't get to keep your guns. She was infinitely more dangerous than a loaded gun.

Claire shut off the audio feed and dimmed the windows. She checked the door. Courtney had engaged the electronic lock. Not enough. A heavy life support unit sat in the corner, for the times when psychers suffered an attack but held on to life. She put her shoulder into it, pushed it across the doorway, barring the door from the inside, and walked past four heads dripping blood back to her seat.

She had to log into the bionet for the last time to erase herself from Brodwyn data systems.

"STEP ONTO THE PLATFORM," a Melko soldier ordered.

Claire obeyed, stepping onto the raised circle in the middle of the room. Six high-caliber gun turrets swiveled on their mounts, locking onto her. To the right and left, two Melko soldiers took aim at her head. Across the room an older woman behind a crescent metal console studied the digital screen.

Three weeks ago she had escaped the Intelligence building and returned to her mother's apartment. It was vacant, like many others, and during her last foray into the Brodwyn bionet, Claire had assigned it to herself. She had resurrected her mother's data and took on her identity, keeping only her name and her date of birth intact. Only her neighbors could have betrayed her. This morning she was arrested with the rest of the residents of the building and marched down to this depot. Nobody spoke out against her.

The older woman peered at her.

"Name?"

"Claire Shannon."

"Occupation?"

"Secretary."

"Do you have any implants, modification, or kinsmen abilities to declare?"

"No."

Claire's mind was hidden behind four layers of solid mental shields, enclosed in a hard outer shell, accreted over the period of the last four weeks as a result of constant mental strain. Her surface thoughts coated this shell, as if it were a mirror. Her defenses would withstand a concentrated probe from an adept. To the outside world, her mind appeared very much alive, but completely inert psychically. Precisely the way she liked it.

"Place your hands on the rail in front of you."

Claire locked her fingers on the metal rail.

Pale green light slid over her. Two dozen scanners recorded her temperature, pulse, and chemical emissions, assessed the composition of the sweat and oil on her fingertips, and probed her body for combat implants.

A cold male voice announced with robotic precision: "Implant scan, class A through E, negative. Biological modification negative."

"Initiating psycher pressure probe," the woman said.

Beneath her mental core, fear washed over Claire. Pressure Probe, PPP, meant pain to a psychic mind. The stronger the psycher, the worse the agony. She had to bear it. Her pulse couldn't speed up. She couldn't wince.

It began as a soft buzz in the back of her skull. The buzz built, ratcheting up to deafening intensity, louder, louder, LOUDER. Pain pierced her mind, as if a drill had carved through the bone, grinding, widening the hole with each rotation, turning her neurons into a mess of human meat. The world dissolved in agony.

She was gone, drowning in pain. Her reason melted. Her mind dissolved.

She gave herself away.

It was over.

The pain vanished, suddenly, as if sliced by a knife.

"PPP negative," the male voice announced.

"Subject cleared the security evaluation," the woman said.

She passed. Somehow she had passed.

The soldiers lowered their weapons.

The woman faced Claire. "You are being deported."

"I'm sorry?"

"We don't want your kind on our planet." The woman grimaced. "You cost us billions and forced us into a three-hundred-year war. If things were fair, we'd line the lot of you up and put you out of your misery, except that the Interplanetary Right to Life Act gets in the way."

That's right, flashed in Claire's mind. She was a civilian and under the protection of the Right to Life Act. Breaking it meant an instant trade embargo. For a planet like Uley that imported most of its food, it would mean a slow death sentence. The Melko retainers couldn't kill her or any of the Brodwyn civilians. They couldn't load them into spaceships and kick them off planet without a definite destination either.

"Melko Corporation made arrangements with other planets to deport you," the woman said. "In your case, you're going to Rada to some kind of flower province. It's one of the merchant planets. Many kinsmen families all competing for their territories. They are cut-throat on Rada and they're only taking the duds like you, no kinsmen allowed. I don't expect you'll last there long, which is just as well. Exit through that door."

Chapter Two

"PPP Negative," the computer announced.

Claire held onto the rail of the platform. She was swimming up a deep well filled with blinding pain. Negative. Negative. She had passed through the screening again.

Please, please let it be for the last time.

"You may leave the platform," Rada's Immigration Officer invited.

She kept swimming. Almost there. Finally she surfaced and her vision returned in a rush. Claire stepped off the platform. The Immigration Officer took her measure. He was lean, dark-haired, and older, his skin either naturally olive or tanned by the sun.

"Come on," he said. "Let me give you your orientation."

She followed him to a small office and sat in the cream-colored chair he indicated. The officer took his place behind a light glass table. A narrow crystal vase sat on the edge of his table. Inside it flowers bloomed, whirl upon whirl of bright petals, some blood red, some yellow, some deep purple near the root of the petal and white at its end. So vivid, almost painful.

"Dahlias," the Immigration officer said.

"I'm sorry?"

"The flowers. They are called dahlias. You are assigned to the city of New Delphi." Behind him the digital screen displayed the city perched at the top of a tall plateau, its sides a sheer cliff of red rock. Elegant skyscrapers of pale white stone, buildings of glass and steel, wider houses with balconies... There was no rhyme or reason to it. Trees grew here and there, bright spots of green. Claire stared.

"New Delphi is the commercial center of the south," the officer said, "but the city itself is located in the Province of Dahlia, hence the flowers. There are other provinces as well. Large urban centers are rare. It's mostly gardens, orchards, family estates. When you hear people speak of 'the provinces,' they are being nostalgic about a less hectic way of life."

The image of the city turned, presenting her with seven long platforms thrusting from the side of the cliff, one above the other, like mushroom ridges on a tree. Tunnels carved into the rock led to the Terraces, probably from somewhere within the city.

"These are the Terraces. This is where you'll find most 'provincial' style restaurants and shops. They are pricier than places in the city but you pay extra for authentic taste. Your apartment is right here."

The image slid down, the buildings rolling by. The picture zoomed in, and she saw a ten-story structure of pale yellow stone. Balconies lined its sides.

"The neighbors from your building are also being placed in this general area. You aren't housed together, because we want you to be assimilated into our culture as soon as possible. But you will see familiar faces. Your apartment is yours for the next three months. That's how long your probation period is. After three months, you must assume the mortgage payments, which means you must find employment."

The image zoomed out before she could catch any more details.

"The city is divided into territories between kinsmen families," the officer continued. "A lot of kinsmen keep private security forces, and a lot of these private soldiers have combat implants. The dominant kinsmen families have vast commercial interests and they often clash, sometimes violently, in an attempt to expand their influence. Duels and assassination attempts are not uncommon. If you see something like that in progress, try to step to the side, out of their way."

"Your people kill each other in the streets?" Unthinkable. How could this be allowed?

"Sometimes. Most kinsmen are so enhanced, the fights rarely last for longer than thirty seconds. Don't worry. They almost never injure bystanders. It would be very rude."

"Rude?" This whole planet was insane.

"Of course. With all of the targeting implants and inborn abilities, they are so fast, you would have to actively work to get in their way. Killing a civilian would be sloppy and the height of bad manners. Our crime rate is low compared to equivalent cities from other planets, and aside from kinsmen settling their affairs, New Delphi's security force has very little tolerance for foolishness. Assaults are rare, crimes like theft and burglary are more frequent. When a criminal commits an illegal act in New Delphi, chances are he's committing it in a territory of some kinsmen family, who will deal with the matter accordingly. Which isn't to say you should go alone into dangerous areas of the city at night or leave your door unlocked."

The officer looked at the screen in front of him. "Your first priority is finding a job. You will receive job recommendations from this office. You must follow these recommendations. Failure to comply will result in deportation to Uley."

"So they aren't really recommendations, are they?" Claire asked.

"No. They are not."

"I see."

"If you fail to obtain a job after five recommendations, you will be downgraded to Class B and recommendations will no longer be provided to you. If you fail to obtain employment within your three-month probation period, you will be deported. If you engage in any criminal activity during your probation period, you will be..."

"...Deported?" Deportation would mean death. Melko Corporation would kill her if she returned. They made it abundantly clear before she boarded the spacecraft.

"We understand each other." The officer nodded again. "Your first job interview is in one hour. When you walk out of this building, you will see a row of aerials. Your aerial is number 57/78. The course is already programmed into it. It will take you to your job interview and then to your apartment. Should you obtain employment, the aerial will return for you in the morning. If you like it, you may choose to assume payments for it at the end of your probation. Here are the particulars." The Immigration Officer slid a data card across the table.

Claire slid it into the tablet she had been issued. The tablet's screen blinked and pale words emerged from the background: Guardian, Inc.: Extrasensory Security Protocols and Biocybernetic Safety.

Her hands went cold. "I'm not a psycher," she managed.

"We know. You show no psychic activity at all." The Immigration officer nodded for emphasis. "The Escana kinsmen family has all the psychers they could want. What they need is support staff with quiet brains, so they can work without interference. They have an Admin Specialist opening and you will apply for it." He peered at her. "Unless there is a problem?"

Passing PPP was one thing. PPP was simply a painful pulse generated by a computer. Walking into a building filled with psychers, whose job it was to find and eradicate psychically active intruders... Declining the recommendation would instantly arouse suspicion. "No problem," Claire said.

"You sure?"

"Yes." Unless one counted certain death as a problem. "I just didn't want to fail before I started."

"Don't worry," the officer said. "You will make an excellent drone."

"May I have your name?" The dark-haired receptionist smiled from behind the counter.

"Claire Shannon," Claire said. The smiles looked odd to her. The aerial had touched down in a parking lot and she had to walk two blocks to the Guardian building. In the five minutes she spent outside, she realized that people of New Delhi spent their lives baring their teeth. They smiled when they opened the door, they smiled when they bought groceries, they smiled if you accidentally happened to meet their gaze on the street. It was deeply unnerving.

"May I ask the purpose of your visit?" the receptionist asked. Behind her on a white stone wall, elegant pale gold letters spelled Guardian, Inc. Under it smaller letters read: Your thoughts are safe with us.

Claire made an effort to smile back. "I'm here to apply for the position of the Administrative Specialist."

A faint touch swept over Claire's mental shield. She held her smile, fighting doubts with logic. She had spent the entire two-week flight reinforcing the shell over her mind and thickening the surface layer. Her mind was well-hidden. Too well, as the interview with the Immigration officer had proved.

"Take the elevator to the fifteenth floor, then follow the hallway," the receptionist said. "You will be met. Good luck!"

"Thank you."

Claire crossed the lobby to the glass elevator, her heels making quiet clicks on the pale granite floor. The presence stayed with her, hovering in the background, scanning her mind, lightly but attentively. Standard practice. People tended to guard themselves during live encounters, such as being questioned by a receptionist. Once past a check point, the body and mind relaxed, and hidden thoughts strayed to the surface. If she was guilty of anything, her relief at having made it this far would be apparent.

She had to appear normal. Most people would be slightly nervous before a job interview and Claire allowed herself some mild anxiety. Nothing out of the ordinary.

The elevator door slid open. Claire stepped inside. The door closed and the aerodynamic cabin accelerated upward.

Shaped like an elongated flower bud, the Guardian Building contained an inner core of offices and working spaces, up the side of which the elevator now climbed. This inner core sat within an outer shell of twisting steel beams forming a diagonal grid, the outer surface of the bud. Solar glass panels sheathed the diagonal spaces between the twisting beams, flooding the inside of the building with a warm golden light that set the polished granite floor of the enormous lobby aglow. The diagrid must've been enormously heavy, but bathed in the sunlight, it seemed ethereal, almost weightless. It was so beautiful, it felt magic.

Her memory served up the recollection of her home world, spare boxes of skyscrapers, canyon streets, her grey apartment, the steel and worn plastic of the spartan spaceship she'd boarded two weeks ago... She couldn't decide if those memories were a nightmare or if this airy building with its bright colors and smiling people in vivid clothes was a lovely delusional dream.

Deep inside, beneath her shields, anxiety churned. Making it to this planet had been a miracle. If her shields failed, she faced immediate deportation. She couldn't go back. Not after seeing this. Besides, if she was deported back to Uley, she'd never make it out of the spaceport. There would be a death squad waiting for her at the spacecraft's door.

Below her, people moved through the lobby. The men wore formfitting black and grey, the women chose flowing dresses and bright colors. What must it be like to come to work here every day? Did they ever become immune to this beauty?

The elevator stopped. Claire sighed, loathe to leave the view behind, turned and exited into a narrow hallway, its indigo, almost black walls reflective like a dark mirror. Above her, long ribbons of dark blue luminescent plastic, set on their edge, ran parallel to each other, curving and twisting like a three-dimensional current of a river. The transparent floor reflected it, and as she walked down the hallway, Claire had an absurd feeling she was swimming.

The hallway opened into a wide chamber, the transparent floor replaced by grey marble. Pale blue and grey couches lined the walls. Three men and two women sat on the couch cushions. Her shield didn't permit her to actively scan their minds, but it didn't prevent her from listening to their psychic emissions. She was open to any signal, like a satellite dish.

The woman on the right, with purple streaks in her black hair, had a loud mind, powerful, but untrained. All her thoughts floated around her like noise above a spaceport. An easy target. The woman on the left was more restrained, but weak. Of the three men, two were trained psychers, but both were mediocre. She had more training by the time she was fifteen. The final man showed no psychic activity at all, his mind practically invisible. On Uley, he would be a dud. Here the term was drone, apparently.

A tall middle-aged woman in an artfully draped, deep red dress stepped through the arched doorway at the end of the room. She was carrying a tablet. The woman looked her over, her gaze precise like the beam of a bio scanner. "Claire Shannon?"

"Yes."

The woman stared at her with brown eyes. Her mind sliced through Claire's surface thoughts with a laser precision and fell short of the shell. That was the beauty of mirroring surface thoughts over the shell - nobody realized the shields were there.

"Take this," the woman said, handing her the tablet. "There are three tests loaded on the tablet. Sit down and complete them. You will be called."

Inwardly, Claire exhaled.

"Rokero Grenali," the woman said.

The older of the men rose and approached her. They disappeared through the doorway.

Claire sat. The polished wall presented her with her own reflection: a severe grey skirt that clasped her narrow waist, a conservative pale blouse, dull brownish hair pulled away from her face. Of the three changes of clothes she was permitted to bring, this was the best, most feminine outfit she owned. She could count on her fingers occasions when she had worn civilian clothes in the last year.

The other two women were looking at her. One wore a slick silvery business suit, the other a vivid red and orange dress. Their minds betrayed their reactions: pity tinged with superiority. They felt prettier. They were bright dahlia blossoms, and she was a drab mouse. They dismissed her.

It hurt. It hurt and stung her pride. The emotions boiled inside and bounced off her inner shields. Her face, reflected in the polished wall, was calm. The outer surface of her mind was collected. Nothing showed except for mild anxiety, typical to any job applicant. She had too much discipline to let any emotion seep through.

She shouldn't have been this unsettled. First the anxiety from the landing, then tests, the echoes of PPP still humming through her skull, and now the realization that she stood out after a lifetime of being told how important it was to perfectly fit in. She attracted too much attention. All those factors shredded her normal poise to tatters. It's the sensory overload, she told herself. It will be fine. She had over eight hundred combat missions behind her. This was just one more.

Claire slid a stylus from its holder on the side of the tablet and scanned the tests. A written and mathematical proficiency, a psychological questionnaire, and a card test. The virtual deck contained fifty-two cards in two sets, one red, one black. Each card bore a single symbol: a circle, a triangle, a diamond, or a long narrow rectangle. The program dealt cards face down and the user had to indicate color and shape. It was the simplest of psychic tests.

She had to make sure she failed it.

"SHANNON," the woman called.

Claire stood up and crossed the now empty hall to the woman in red. She was the last applicant of the day. Her chances of being hired had shrunk to miniscule.

"My name is Lienne," the woman informed her. "Follow me."

They crossed through another dark hall. Claire braced herself. Whoever waited for her would scour her mind. Her shields had to hold.

They entered a large room. To the left, a floor to ceiling window showed the view of the diagrid envelope, the light streaming through the solar panels now the deep honey of late afternoon. Three plush crescent-shaped couches formed a ring in the middle of the room with a cream-colored coffee table made of reflective plasti-glass in the center. Further, a crescent desk of the same material curved from the wall, on which a large screen hung, streaming some sort of data. A tall blond man stood with his back to her. He turned at their approach and Claire almost stumbled.

He had a strong, masculine face, with a square clean-shaven jaw. On Uley, blond people had a washed out, sickly look, their skin too white, their hair verging on transparent. His skin was flawless bronze, his hair a pale, almost white gold. His broad shoulders strained the fabric of his tailored light-grey summer doublet, the outline of muscle on his chest and arms plainly visible under the thin fabric. Everything about him, from the way he turned, graceful and perfectly balanced, to the way he held himself now, communicated health, strength, and power. He was sun-kissed, golden, overwhelming.

His dark green eyes focused on her, reflecting a sharp, perceptive intellect. The eyes of a man who could be either very generous or completely ruthless. The man smiled, at once charming and reassuring, and she felt the power of his mind. It was like a typhoon held back, enclosed in a self-imposed cage.

It was too much. Every coping mechanism that had let her make it this far collapsed. She stared with no idea how to respond.

He was larger than life.

Lienne cleared her throat.

The sound shattered her trance. Claire closed her mouth.

"You're Claire," the man said, his voice resonant, communicating strength as much as his body did.

"Yes?" she answered, reeling from the shock.

"My name is Venturo Escana," he said.

The Escana kinsman family, a distant part of her mind informed her. They owned Guardian, Inc., and Venturo Escana led the family. She was facing the god of this beautiful building.

"This is my aunt, Lienne Escana; she is my second in command. Please sit down," he invited her to the couch.

She sat on autopilot, smoothing her skirt over her legs. She felt so out of place here, in this office. Venturo sat across from her. Lienne sat on the same couch as he, leaving several feet between them.

"You're a refugee," he said.

She couldn't sit there, mute, and simply stare. Claire forced herself to formulate words. "Yes."

"As I understand, our planet made an arrangement with your home world. We agreed to accept a certain number of refugees in return for the use of Uley's interstellar bases as refuel points. I understand your home world made these arrangements with a number of other planets."

"That's correct," she said. He was keeping his mind firmly away from hers. It was an exquisitely polite gesture. She had expected him to batter her the moment she entered the room.

"It must've been very difficult to leave your world."

He had no idea. "I've been very fortunate to arrive here."

"Do you like it here?" he asked with genuine interest.

"It's very beautiful," she said. "Very bright." Too bright. Too vivid. Too many smiles. Men that were... that were...

"We try to live life to its fullest," he said.

He didn't intend anything sexual by it, but inside her shields, his words triggered an image of him naked. It flashed before her, stunning in its shamelessness. She wanted to touch him.

I'm losing my mind.

"I suppose we have to begin the interview now," he said, almost apologetic. "It's important that you answer with complete honesty. Lienne and I are monitoring your thoughts. We will be able to detect a lie."

His mind touched hers, very gently. She held absolutely still, terrified that any of her runaway emotions would break out of her shields.

"Don't be nervous," he told her. "It will be fine, I promise."

She concentrated on the table in front of her, crushing her sexual impulses and painting calm over her emotions.

"What did you do on your home world?" he asked.

"I was a secretary at a munitions factory," she lied. "We manufactured parts for the long range coastal guns." It was her cover. When asked what she did outside of the Psych Corps, she was supposed to respond with this line.

"What made you decide to apply to become a retainer of the Escana family?" he asked.

"It was recommended to me by the Immigration Service," she said, relieved to be honest. "As a condition of my deportation, I'm required to follow the employment recommendation." Even when it's cosmic irony.

"Your anxiety level is rising," Venturo said. "Why?"

Claire swallowed. Complete honesty. "I'm afraid."

"What scares you?" he asked.

"I'm afraid I will be deported if I fail the interview." It was the truth.

"As a refugee, you have five chances to obtain employment before you will face the possibility of deportation," Lienne said, her voice crisp.

"It's not a completely rational fear," Claire said.

"Why did the Immigration Service recommend Guardian, Inc. as a prospective employer?" Venturo asked.

"I was tested and it was determined that I have no psychic ability whatsoever. The Immigration officer said that your company prefers to employ non-psychics for its support staff to lessen the telepathic interference. He said that I would make an excellent drone."

A shadow darkened Venturo's eyes. His mind shifted subtly, and she glimpsed the hint of steel will that drove it. All of his pleasant demeanor aside, Venturo Escana would make a terrifying enemy.

"That's not a word we favor," he said.

"My apologies."

"Not your fault." Venturo held out his hand and Lienne put a tablet into his fingers. "What was it you say you did?"

He remembered perfectly well what she told him. She aligned her thoughts. "I was an administrative assistant. I answered phones..." She recalled answering a phone at a desk and projected it onto the surface of her mind.

"...I took messages..."

A memory of writing things down.

"...I prepared reports..."

A memory of sitting before a screen filling out a long form.

She had served as a secretary a week out of the year specifically to be able to recall these memories if questioned.

"You are an admin," Venturo said. "Your boss is out of touch. A customer calls. He is angry. There was a mistake in his bill. Your move."

"Ask the customer to tell me in detail about the problem, taking notes along the way. Assure the customer that I will do everything in my power to resolve the issue and promise to let him know as soon as the solution is found. Follow the company protocol to initiate an inquiry into the case."

"Why not just transfer him to Billing?" Venturo asked. "It's their mistake."

"Or wait for the return of your employer," Lienne said.

"An irate customer wants someone to listen to him," Claire said. "If his grievances are heard, the conflict is eliminated. Once I transfer him to Billing, I lose control of the situation. I have no way of knowing how Billing will treat him. And while I will inform my employer of the situation, if the situation can be resolved without his direct involvement, why not resolve it?"

Venturo and Lienne shared a look.

"Your employer's wife enters your office, demanding to see him. She is visibly angry," Lienne said. "Your employer is in a meeting."

"Request security assistance via silent alarm. Ascertain that no life-threatening emergency is in progress and attempt to diffuse the situation. If the spouse proves uncooperative, let security escort her out."

"But she is your employer's wife," Lienne said.

"My job is to make sure my employer can function at maximum capacity. The presence of his angry wife would hinder the operation of the company."

"So you automatically assume the worst and push the alarm?" Venturo asked.

She had a feeling she wasn't giving them the answer they were looking for. "I must anticipate what an angry spouse could do rather than what she is likely to do. She may be simply angry, or she might have a weapon in her purse. If I can convince the spouse to leave the premises peacefully, security would have wasted a few minutes of their time. But if the spouse becomes unreasonable or violent, and I fail to anticipate it, people might become injured."

"An employee calls you in a panic to tell you there is a fire on the floor below," Venturo said.

"Alert authorities and initiate immediate evacuation," Claire said.

Venturo frowned.

She scrutinized her answer, wishing she could touch his mind and try to figure out what she had done wrong. It was the obvious answer. She could think of no alternative.

Venturo leaned back, frowning. A focused thought dashed from him toward Lienne, and Claire caught it. His mind was like the beam of a lighthouse.

"Opinion?"

"She would make a terrible admin," Lienne answered. *"Her thought patterns are consistent with that of an executive. She accepts personal responsibility for every issue. Her answers to the questionnaire demonstrate the same thing."*

Inwardly Claire clenched. She'd stumbled. The military conditioning finally betrayed her.

"You're looking at the product of a seventy-year war," Venturo's mind said. *"She evaluates her environment for threats and defuses them. It's a useful quality."*

Lienne sighed mentally. *"Oh no. Ven, please don't tell me you found another lost puppy?"*

Claire studied her hands. Lost puppy...

"What if the next firm she goes to rejects her as well? Eventually she will be deported. Have you seen the images of that place? It's hell."

"I've read the coverage, too. Chemical warfare, casualties in thousands, and everyone with a drop of kinsmen blood turned into a killer. We have no way of verifying who she is or what she is capable of besides what Immigration tells us. This is a terrible idea."

"No kinsman *would have made it through the immigration screening. Her mind is completely inert. What harm can she do? Look at it as a good deed for the day."*

In her mind Lienne smiled. *"Are you sure you're hiring her because you're buying her hard luck story and not because she looks at you as if you're made of gold?"*

They knew. They both realized her reaction to him. It must've been so apparent, a blind man could've seen it. How embarrassing.

"Hire her," Venturo's thought communicated. *"I can make a difference in her life today and I intend to do so."*

"Then let me put her as one of the junior assistants. As your admin, she would be representing the company. I mean, look at her, Venturo. She looks like a beggar. That hair... The woman obviously has never been inside a salon in her entire life..."

Deep inside her shell, Claire pictured slapping Lienne's mind. The older woman was powerful, but not powerful enough. One slap and Lienne would wake up on the floor an hour or so later, unsure how she got there.

Venturo's mind focused on his aunt. It wasn't a gesture designed to intimidate; he simply "stared" at her, but the force of that mental "look" was nearly overwhelming. Like standing in the path of an avalanche.

Mentally Lienne bowed her head. "As you wish."

Venturo held his aunt in the sniper scope of his mental stare for another long second and glanced back at her. "Claire, how much do you know about extrasensory security?"

"Nothing." Everything.

"Most of the computers we use are simply a collection of mechanical parts," he said. "However, certain corporations and government systems require a higher level of data processing. They run on biological networks. These networks are vulnerable to psychic attacks. We provide security for these systems. If you choose to work here, you will have to sign a confidentiality agreement. You cannot discuss the nature of your work with anyone. Will that be an issue for your family?"

"I have no family."

"You do have a place to stay?" he asked.

"Yes. Immigration provided me with an apartment."

"Good," he said. "You're hired. Lienne will take care of the details."

"Thank you," she whispered.

"You're welcome." He rose and walked away to his desk. Lienne stood up and gave her a pointed glance. Claire followed her outside through the hallway into the outer office. Lienne tapped her tablet and held her hand to the slit in the recessed wall to their right. The wall spat a narrow ring of deep red into her palm.

"Hand," the woman ordered.

Claire held out her hand and Lienne slid the ring on her right middle finger. "Two weeks advance. It will be recouped gradually from your pay. Squeeze the sides to view the balance." The older woman examined her critically. "New wardrobe. Nothing too provocative, nothing too drab. Nothing like this." She indicated Claire's clothes with the sweep of her hand.

It wasn't an insult, but it felt like a slap. "Thank you," Claire said.

"You will be replacing Olemi, Venturo's personal admin. If it was up to me, I would place you in a position of lesser responsibility, but he insisted. He will see every mistake you will make and I have no doubt he will overlook some of them, because he is a kind man. But his patience isn't infinite." Steel laced Lienne's gaze. "Make no mistake, Claire. If you betray our family, he will kill you."

"I understand." He would find her a surprisingly difficult target.

"This tablet contains the work manuals that explain your duties and company procedures. Ven feels sorry for you. Going through life relying on the sympathy of strangers is no way to live. I suggest you memorize these manuals over the weekend, so you can earn your keep with something more than your sad story." Lienne pursed her lips. "Do you have any questions?"

"Would it be a problem if I dyed my hair?"

Lienne arched her eyebrows. "Dictating the color of your hair would violate Employee Rights. I can tell you what clothes to wear, but clothes can be removed at the end of the work day. Hair cannot. You may dye it whatever shade you wish, although I would hope that it will be something tasteful. Working here is a privilege even for the most qualified applicants. You've been given a gift. Don't waste it."

CLAIRE SLID into the seat of the aerial. She felt lost, as if her very being was unravelling at the seams and the tatters of her psyche swirled around her, lifted by the breeze.

"Destination?" an automated male voice asked.

"Find a salon frequented by businesswomen."

"The closest location is Allure. Eighty-six percent of users provided four star or above rating. Estimated time of travel: ten minutes. Permission to book an appointment?"

"Book it."

The aerial hummed and took to the air. Claire slumped on the seat. A lost puppy. She was Venturo Escana's rescued mongrel. The handsome golden man felt sorry for her. He knew that he stunned her and he felt pity for her. Her pride didn't just sting, it twisted in contortions. She wanted to crack her shell open, show him the full power of her mind, and scream, "Look at me!"

They would throw her off planet so fast, she wouldn't have a chance to blink.

Fatigue flowed over her in a heavy wave.

She had a job. She had an apartment. No matter how bad it was, it had to be better than the concrete box on Uley.

She tapped the tablet and pulled up the employee manual. Bionet protocols. Basic security. Data compilation. She could do this job in her sleep. She had done it sixteen years ago - that's how all psychers started.

She would have to make sure that she made small insignificant mistakes to avoid calling attention to her sudden expertise.

"You have reached your destination," the aerial announced. They landed. She stepped out of the vehicle. In front of her, a building rose, shaped like an ancient ivory hand fan, complete with lace carved in wide panes. The sign above the rectangular doorway proclaimed Allure.

Claire walked inside. The glass doors hissed open at her approach. At the receptionist desk a man with lemony yellow hair glanced at her.

"I have an appointment," she said.

"Claire?"

"Yes." She could see her own reflection in the mirror behind him: pale brown hair of interminable shade, pulled back from her face into a braid, generously streaked with premature gray and tinted with slight orange.

"What will it be?"

She pointed to her hair. "Fix this."

Thirty seconds later she sat in a chair. A woman approached her. "Good afternoon, my name is Belina and what will we... oh my. Horatio?"

A slight, effeminate man approached, wiping his hands with a towel. "Take the braid out."

Belina unwound the braid and her hair fell around Claire's face in a dense wave.

"Better already." Horatio leaned next to her, looking in the mirror at her reflection. "Why is it stained with orange?" he asked softly.

"Chemical deposits in the water," she said.

"I see. What will you let us do?"

"I've been hired as an admin by the Escana family," she said. "You may do anything that won't get me fired."

Two hours later Claire looked in the mirror. The woman who looked back was about five years younger. A cloud of copper-red hair fell on her shoulders in an artful cascade, glinting with splashes of gold and deep red, softening her features and bringing out her grey eyes. She turned her head, and the hair moved, shimmering and light. Claire studied the woman's face. It didn't belong to her.

"Gorgeous," Horatio said as she settled the bill and she smiled back at him without forcing it.

"Where do business women shop?" she asked him.

"How much money do you have?"

She squeezed the ring, checking. "Two thousand credits."

He borrowed her tablet and scribbled the address with a stylus. "Ask for Sophia. And use the shampoo I gave you. Red fades fast."

By the time the aerial finally landed in front of her apartment, the sky had grown dark. Claire ducked into the entrance and walked up the stairs to the fourth floor. She pressed her thumb to the keypad. The lock clicked open, and she stepped inside.

Walls of warm inviting yellow greeted her. The floor was textured tile in a dozen shades of pale green, brown, and beige. Soft green couches waited to be sat on to her right. A curved coffee table carved from some reddish rock rested between them, and on it in a wide glass dish floated burgundy-red dahlia blossoms. Ahead, double doors framed by diaphanous curtains led to a balcony.

Claire dropped her bags.

The apartment was completely quiet. She walked across the floor to the door and slid it open. A small balcony presented her with a view of the sunset: above her the cosmos was deep purple and far ahead, at the horizon, where the setting sun rolled behind the distant mountains, the sky glowed with bright vivid red. Wind fanned her, bringing with it a scent of some flower she didn't know.

She sat down on the floor of the balcony, behind the trellised rail, and cried.

Chapter Three

Claire opened her eyes. The ceiling above her was cream, painted with yellow stripes from the rays of the morning sun filtering through the window.

She rolled out of bed and walked out onto the balcony. Outside, New Delphi buzzed with life. In the sky, crisscrossing currents of aerials flowed one above the other, sliding toward the distant buildings of the business sector. Below, a wide street led into the distance, framed by buildings in every color, shape, and size. People strolled on the sidewalk. Claire watched a young woman leading two little girls down the street. Both children wore flowing white dresses and straw hats with small flowers in the brim. Their little sandals made loud slapping sounds on the sidewalk: flop, flop, flop. The woman stopped at a small stall offering buckets of fruit under a bright green awning. The vendor offered the little girls a cup of some sort of round red berries.

Suddenly she was starving.

Claire rummaged through the new clothes she'd hung up in the closet, found a simple pale blue dress, slipped it on, and ran out the door.

The street vendor was old, his hair almost completely grey, his nose large with a bump, like a beak of some bird. He squinted at her with dark eyes as she looked at the fruit.

"What's this one?" she pointed to a bulbous green fruit.

"Pears," he said.

"And this one?" She pointed at the big sphere of yellow blushing with red on one side.

"Dahlia peaches."

Claire picked up a peach and smelled. The delicate, sweet aroma teased her.

"You're from Uley?" he asked.

She nodded.

"I've seen a few of you in the neighborhood," he said. "You're braver than most. Usually it takes your people ten minutes to decide to talk to me." He pointed to boxes one by one. "This one is sweet but firm, this one is sweet and soft, this one is tart..."

"One of each," she said and held her ring to the scanner mounted on the stall's support.

"We can do that."

The vendor took a satchel from a stack and filled it with fruit, sliding it carefully into the bag one by one.

A brush of a familiar mind made Claire turn. A woman approached, her dark hair pulled back into a bun. She wore a familiar grey tunic of simple cut over plain trousers. Tonya Damon, Claire remembered. She lived across from her mother's apartment.

Tonya saw her and halted, awkward. The look of worry in the woman's eyes stabbed at Claire. She'd seen this reaction before: she was a psycher, an officer, and a killer and Tonya was afraid.

"Are you here for the fruit?" Claire asked, forcing a smile.

"Yes. No. I was just looking."

Claire took the satchel from the vendor's hand and pulled out a pear. "Would you like to try one?"

Tonya looked at the pear.

"I got carried away and bought a whole bag," Claire said.

"She did," the vendor confirmed.

Tonya swallowed.

"I can't possibly eat it all by myself. It would be a waste."

She'd said the magic word. Tonya reached out for the pear and took it. "Thank you."

"You're welcome."

Tonya hesitated.

Claire waited, the smile in place.

"When did you arrive?" Tonya said finally.

"Yesterday. You?"

"A week ago." The woman blinked. "I found a job. I work for a chemical laboratory. That's what I did on Uley, so it worked out."

"That's great," Claire told her. "I found a job, too, as an admin."

"That's nice." Tonya smiled.

What was her husband's name... "How's Mark?"

"Mark died," Tonya said. "Killed on the front line two years ago."

"I'm so sorry."

"That's alright. It was nice to see you."

"Nice to see you as well. I live in that building over there." Claire nodded at the apartment. "Fourth floor. If you need anything..."

"I'm down the street. I better go. Thank you for talking to me."

"Thank you."

Tonya turned, took a few hurried steps, turned and came closer. She licked her lips, unsure, leaned closer and said, her voice barely above a whisper. "Your hair is too bright."

She ducked her head and hurried on, the pear in her hand.

"What was that all about?" the vendor asked.

"It's a kindness," Claire said. "She was trying to save me from embarrassment, because my hair draws attention."

"Don't listen to her. I like your hair," the vendor said. "It's sunny."

"I like my hair too. Thank you for the fruit." She took the satchel and went to her apartment.

Claire washed the fruit, arranged it on a plastic cutting board she'd found in the kitchen and took it and a knife to the coffee table. She cut the fruit into slices, put it into a bowl and took it to the couch. She linked her tablet to the larger digital screen on the wall and pulled up the work manuals. The Guardian procedure differed slightly from Uley's military protocols but the basic methods were the same. She'd finished with them and looked at the screen.

She still had a lot of fruit and nothing to do.

"Net search: Venturo Escana."

"Venturo Escana," the AI announced in a pleasant male voice. "Son of Haldor Madsen and Malvina Escana. Founder and joint owner of Guardian, Inc. Personal net worth estimated at seven million credits -"

"No audio," she said. "I want to read it."

The digital screen flashed, opening various news articles. She scooted deeper into the couch and reached for a piece of some green fruit shaped like an ancient hour-glass.

She sifted through press releases, financial statements, and tabloid gossip. There wasn't much. Guardian, Inc., seemed to have a stellar reputation. In the eight years of its existence, the firm had grown from a small start-up to the third largest provider of bionet security in the southern hemisphere. Its chief competitors, Apex and DSS, both had decades of experience and a lot of family capital backing them up.

The entire Escana family preferred to fly under the radar. All she found were random images of Venturo in a formal setting in the company of New Delphi's elite, usually escorting a beautiful woman. She tried to narrow down his type. He seemed to show no preference. The only common ground between his dates consisted of expensive tastes, beauty, and superior grooming.

Studying New Delphi's movers and shakers proved highly educational. There was no color too bright or inappropriate for clothes or hair. She ended up laughing at the ridiculous dresses and insane shoes. It was the best time she'd had in the last decade.

A small link popped up on the screen in the corner. She

followed it to an eighteen-year-old news item. "Rumors of Engagement between de Solis and Escana."

Hmm. Now that was interesting, since that de Solis owned DDS.

"The persistent rumors of a union between de Solis and Escana kinsmen families can be put to rest. When asked for comment, Castilla de Solis debunked all speculation of the proposed engagement between herself and Venturo Escana. It seems the de Solis heiress holds the rising star of the Escana clan in low regard. Had the rumors proven true, the struggling Escana Family would have reaped great financial benefits..."

"Castilla de Solis, image," Claire said.

A picture of a woman filled the screen. Tall, slender, athletic, she leaned back, laughing, the bright lavender dress falling off her shoulders, held up seemingly by her breasts alone. Jet black hair spilled down her back in a glossy wave.

No way to gauge her psycher capacity.

If that was Venturo's type, she'd chosen the wrong hair color. She should've dyed her hair black.

Claire leaned back. "Delete."

Castilla disappeared, replaced by an image of Venturo: golden, muscular, his green eyes sharp with intellect. Her body tightened in response, eager for contact. She imagined sliding her hands along those carved arms...

Claire exhaled slowly. There was no rational explanation why when she looked at him, she thought of sex. It was an involuntary response, completely at odds with her personality and training.

Sex was a means of relief. On Uley, it was an understood fact that one engaged in it, but it was rarely discussed. She had a sexual partner once. His name was Dominic. She was eighteen, he was twenty-two. She had just made lieutenant and he was in line for the captain promotion. They had three months together and in those three months she had something to look forward to when she returned to her apartment. She could still recall the feel of his hands on her, the way he said her name, the way he felt inside her.

The Intelligence had transferred him across the city. They had no warning. One day he was simply gone. It didn't take her long to put it together: she was a rising star and he was perceived as a distraction. He didn't try to look for her. He didn't put up a fight. Since then, she'd kept her sexual impulses under lock and key. Masturbation brought her the same relief, and while it came with no intimacy, it didn't carry a burden of disappointment either. In her last weeks on Uley she hadn't even felt the need for it.

She looked at Venturo Escana on the screen. It was as if some vital part of her, the one that was female and craved male contact, sex, and love, had withered. Somehow this man had managed to resuscitate it without doing anything at all. And he felt nothing except pity for her. The irony made her laugh.

She would see him again on Monday. She had to make sure to not make a fool of herself.

HER SUPERVISOR WAS a woman three years her junior. Her name was Renata, her hair was dark brown, her nails bright yellow, and when she was surprised, she opened her brown eyes so wide, she looked slightly deranged.

"How did you get through these so fast?"

"I'm motivated." Claire smiled.

Renata scrolled through the bionet activity reports with rows of tabled data. "Hang on, I have to find something to gripe about." She kept scrolling. "Oh. Here, look, the Radon sector heading should be in blue and you have it in grey." Her fingers flew over her keyboard. "Fix, fix, fix! Fixed."

Claire studied Renata out of the corner of her eye. Her mannerisms were so... carefree. Not exactly childlike but completely devoid of the somber poise common to Uley. If you dropped Renata, the big smile, wide eyes, and purple dress, in the middle of an Uley skyscraper, people would pretend she wasn't there. They'd just refuse to see her. Maybe some well-meaning soul would walk up to her and confidentially inform her that her hair was too bright and she was making a fool of herself...

A mental tug interrupted Claire's musings. Venturo Escana, approaching fast. A walking mental firestorm of a mind behind an invisible wall of steel will.

"All set." Renata raised her hands from the keys. "Did you review the Sangori file?"

"Yes." Venturo's mind was coming closer.

"And the recommendations?

"Yes."

"Good! Be ready to spit it all back at Ven when he comes by. He has a meeting with them later this afternoon and he prefers the spoken summary. But don't worry, he knows most of the file already. He just needs a refresher course."

He had a heightened auditory focus - his mind processed sound better than visual cues. Although for most people the theory of learning styles had long been debunked, for psychers it remained true: some were visual learners, some listened, and others had to write every scrap of information down. She'd worked with auditory psychers like that before. There was a trick to it - the combination of the correct intonation, vocabulary, and the information presented in a logical manner.

Renata's eyes widened. "Speak of the devil."

Venturo had turned the corner. Claire braced herself and turned to look, slowly.

The amicable man she saw yesterday was gone. He wore a black shirt that clung to him like paint, focusing attention on every contoured muscle. A fine mesh of hair-thin fibers snaked its way through the fabric, widening into oblong scales on his chest and the larger muscles of his shoulders. He looked as if he wore armor, if armor could be flexible and form-fitting. His eyes were dark, and his mind churned - something occupied his attention. He moved with purpose, striding straight down the hallway with a kind of fierce masculine determination. People moved out of his way.

"What is he wearing?" Claire murmured.

"A bionet suit. When psychers log into the net, their bodies don't move at all. A human body isn't designed to be completely immobile unless it floats," Renata said. "The suits start pulsing after a while, exercising the muscles and making sure lymph keeps moving."

A bionet suit. Claire recalled waking up cramped up after hours in the bionet and wincing as the medic massaged her limbs back into life.

"Someone's smitten," Renata said.

Claire glanced at her. "Is it that obvious?"

"Yes. Very." Renata paused. "Claire, you do know what psychers do, don't you?"

She needed to give a general answer. "Provide security?"

"If they catch hackers on the bionet, they kill them." Renata leaned closer. "Venturo's death count is in the dozens. You can't keep doing that sort of work and not be affected."

You don't say.

"He looks delicious and golden, but his head is a dark place. He was attacked in front of our building once - four people - and he drove each of them to impale themselves on an iron fence, one by one. You don't need to tangle with that kind of mind. Trust me on this."

"I understand," Claire said.

"There is a reason why psychers in Guardian, Inc. aren't permitted to read our minds. Sometimes a two-way connection happens and you see things in their heads. Dark things. He's a kinsman - all they care about is power and influence. Not to mention that nothing serious could ever come from it. Psychers love other psychers. Something about joining of the minds, and all that."

Venturo saw them. His steps sped up a fraction.

Renata fell silent.

Claire looked down at her tablet.

Venturo stopped by them. "Renata, where is the new hire? The refugee?"

Claire glanced up. Renata cleared her throat and pointed at Claire with her stylus. Venturo turned. His eyes narrowed.

For a brief, tiny second the two of them were alone in the universe, and then he nodded. "Love the hair. I need the summary of the Sangori file."

He turned and stalked into his office.

Renata jerked her head in the direction of his retreating back and mouthed, "Go."

Claire smiled inwardly and followed.

Venturo landed in his chair, his face dark, and leaned back, hands on the arm rest. The door slid shut, sealing them off from the rest of the offices. Claire sat.

"Sangori File," Claire began, enunciating clearly to let him tag it in his head. "Principals: Savien Sangori, head of the family, sixty-two years old, grey hair, stocky build, tendency to lick his lips when he is nervous."

"Was this in the file?" he asked.

"This was in the news footage which I watched this morning. It was recorded when he was interviewed last year in connection with insider trading."

He nodded. "Continue."

"Maureen Sangori, wife of Savien, fifty-seven years old, dark hair, lean, combat implant of at least B level. Prefers knives. Quick to anger. Likes the color white: white dress, white flowers, white aerial..."

It took her about an hour to recite the Sangori file. Sangori Finances, the investment concern with a net worth of one point two billion credits, had grown too large for the common computing solutions. The firm was preparing to switch to the bionet by launching a new incarnation of the management system that allowed their clients instant access to their portfolio. They were in desperate need of a bionet safety solution and Guardian, Inc. was happy to provide them with one.

Venturo listened with his eyes closed without interruptions. There was always a chance that she had miscalculated, but most psychers perceived and processed the information similarly. She had presented it the way her own mind analyzed it, except she preferred her cues to be visual.

"End file," she said.

Venturo opened his eyes.

A digital screen chimed. "Sangori appointment in twenty minutes, Red Conference Room."

Ven stood up, went to the door, and paused by Renata's desk. "Take her off routine processing."

"For how long?" Renata asked.

"Until further notice." Ven started down the hallway and turned, walking backward. "Come on."

Claire pointed at herself. "Me?"

"Who else?"

She caught up with him. "Where are we going?"

"To my Sangori appointment. I may need another point of view."

She hid a grin and followed him into the elevator.

Chapter Four

Claire strode down the hallway, her heels clicking lightly on the transparent floor, her tablet in her hand. She wore a pale green dress that set off her hair and her new tan. The day was winding down, and the week with it.

The hallway brought her to thirty-three twelve, a wide room nicknamed the Wheel. The Wheel consisted of a round common area from which a dozen office rooms branched in a circle. From above it looked like a flower with a circular middle and elongated petals.

People emerged from the offices at her approach. Hands held out pseudopapers and data strips. She was a link to Ven and everyone wanted to get their bit in before the Friday rolled to a close.

"Earnings projections for the next twin-week!"

"What do you want me to do about the Vinogradov case?" Marto asked.

"He will look at it this afternoon," she replied.

"What about Hawk Corp.?" Liana asked.

"Monday." Claire smiled.

"Here's the Bodia summary."

When she made it to the lift, her hands were full. No matter how well Venturo treated his employees and how ethical he was in keeping his mind to himself, the non-psychers never could get rid of a nagging suspicion that he might be scanning their thoughts. She'd been on the receiving end of these suspicions before: people who went out of their way to avoid her, never discourteous but always cautious. It made her isolated. Psychers stuck together, because the rest of the world was rarely welcoming.

Claire turned and watched the sun shine through the solar panels as the elevator moved upward. In the month she had spent as Venturo's assistant, she had managed to become an indispensable link between him and the support staff. They saw her as safe, a buffer between them and Venturo's lethal brain. It was at once so much more than she thought she would achieve and so much less than she was capable of.

The doors whispered open, and she exited the elevator, heading for Venturo's office. It was Friday. The weekend was just around the corner.

Having two days off after a lifetime of weekends consisting of half-days on Sunday seemed like a decadent luxury. The first three weekends she slept, tried take-out from the neighboring restaurants, and watched broadcasts, soaking up information about the Province of Dahlia like a sponge. She'd finally decided she had enough understanding of the customs and planned to venture to the Terraces this weekend.

She saw him through the translucent door at the end of the hallway: he stood by his desk, his wide back to her, talking to a digital screen, the line of his shoulders tense. Something unpleasant.

Things with Venturo had become progressively more complicated. She no longer stared in stunned silence when she saw him, but as they worked together, the facets of his personality became apparent. Venturo had a fierce intellect and a relentless drive to succeed, knitted together by a kind of arrogance evolved from understanding your own power.

Venturo had definite ideas about how things had to be and he held himself to these strict standards. In the month she had acted as his personal aide, she had seen him furious over a stupid mistake an employee had made, yet when the same employee meekly came to the slaughter, Venturo treated him with tact and flawless politeness. On two occasions, Ven ran around the building, trying to hide from his aunt and an invitation to some family function, until Lienne lost her patience and turned her mind into a glowing beacon of light, mind-scanning the place for him, but in their interactions he would be respectful to her without fail.

It was this control that drew her in. The more she learned about him, the more she was drawn to him. That and the small, seemingly insignificant things he did for her. He opened the door for her. She had discovered that the drink machine in the Wheel dispensed tea in thirty different flavors, and after a hard day of work, when Ven would make his evening pilgrimage to get himself a coffee, he would bring her a cup of hot tea. He sought her opinion, and he would ask her seemingly random things. Did she have a chance to go to the Botanical Gardens? Has she been to the Terraces?

He must've been something else on the bionet. She would never know. He would never see her on the bionet either.

Lucky for her, her ability to control her emotions was never in question. She was never less than professional in their interactions.

The office door slid open. Claire stepped inside.

Venturo turned. She read fury in his eyes. His mind churned and broiled. "We're about to lose the Sangori account."

What? "To whom?" she asked.

"De Solis Security."

DSS. Guardian's biggest rival.

Claire reviewed the facts. Bionet safety consisted of two phases: the establishment and the maintenance. The establishment meant installation of static security mechanisms and structuring the bionet in a way that would lead an intruder into these defenses. The maintenance consisted of responding to active threats. Of the two, the establishment phase was the most costly and the most labor-intensive. Because of the danger involved, the maintenance brought in a larger amount of money but required fewer man-hours.

Venturo had given the Sangori a very good deal on the establishment to entice them into employing Guardian, Inc. He had been planning to recoup his costs on the maintenance fees.

The contract had been signed. They'd been working on the establishment phase for the past three weeks and it was completed this morning. Giving it up would mean DSS would reap all of the benefits of their groundwork.

A clause in the contract gave Sangori legal means to terminate it after the establishment. The clause was standard, but in every meeting with Venturo and Savien, the head of the Sangori family, had asserted his intention to continue with the maintenance phase. He broke his word.

The anger in Ven's mind told her they had no legal recourse.

"How much do we stand to lose?" she asked.

"Two million credits," he said. "It's not the money."

"I don't understand," she said.

"Savien Sangori doesn't have the expertise to engineer this scheme on his own. He knows money; he doesn't understand the bionet. This took a psycher, someone who had looked at the amount of work involved and quoted him exact numbers prior to him ever walking into my building. DDS has conspired with him. They must've offered him monthly maintenance at a lower price if he managed to get the establishment out of me. They set us up."

Now she understood. "It's about pride then."

He faced her. "Yes. More, it's about business. I've been double-crossed. Suckered like a fool. I provide security. Would you want a gullible fool to protect your data?"

"A psycher's gullibility has no bearing on the destructive potential of his mind." She almost bit the last word. She shouldn't have said that.

Ven looked at her, his mind focusing on hers. If he looked too closely, she would be outed.

"Forgive me," Claire said. "I've been trying to read some research in my spare time. I may have misunderstood."

He considered it for a long second and let it go.

"You understand perfectly," he said. "But not many other people do."

He pulled his doublet off the back of his chair.

"Where are you going?"

"To have a conversation with Savien Sangori. I'm going to attempt to explain the facts of life to him."

"Those facts being?" she asked.

"I make a dangerous enemy," he said, "and Sangori is an old provincial family. They have never before betrayed the integrity of their family name to make a credit. I'm curious why they decided to start now."

"What if he refuses to talk to you?"

"I'm not planning on giving him a chance to decline."

Alarm dashed through her. She set her pseudopapers in the chair and plucked her tablet out from the bottom of the stack.

"What are you doing?" he asked.

"I'm coming with you."

"Why?"

"Because you shouldn't go alone."

He peered at her, incredulous. "And you're planning to come as my bodyguard?"

"I am."

It would take her at least three minutes to break through the shell over her mind, bringing her to combat readiness. It would be an eternity in a psycher fight, where death was instant. Still, she couldn't let him go alone and she didn't need to listen to his mind to realize he wouldn't take anyone he considered capable of delivering damage to watch his back. Venturo Escana, arrogant beast that he was, would consider backup beneath him.

"Just out of purely academic curiosity, how exactly are you planning to defend me?" Ven asked. "You have no weapons, no combat enhancements, and your mind is inert. Are you planning on beating Sangori's assassins off with that tablet or were you thinking of a more theoretical approach? Should I look forward to you giving me a detailed analysis of a knife sticking out of my back? If I happen to die, will you deliver a slide point presentation describing my valor at my funeral?"

"Are you finished?"

"Possibly."

"Very well." She raised her chin. "I'm ready when you are."

"You do realize that this is foolish?"

She simply looked at him, loading her gaze with as much scorn and sarcasm as she could manage.

As they were walking down the hallway, Ven leaned to her. "Thank you."

"You're welcome. I hope you don't get us killed."

"They wouldn't dare touch you," he said. "You're a noncombatant."

They stepped into the elevator.

"Can you kill outside of the bionet?" she asked.

"If the Sangori are smart, you will never have to find out," he said.

VEN MARCHED into the lobby of Sangori Investments. Claire followed him, a step behind. Inside, white columns rose up, five stories tall and lit from the inside with a warm yellow light. An ornate lacy relief of vines and flowers sheathed the columns, blocking the illumination, so the spaces between leaves and flowers glowed with white. Delicate golden chairs sat in groups by ornate tables, so airy they might have been spun by spiders. People occupying the chairs chatted in quiet voices.

In the back of the lobby, a reception area waited, flanked by shorter columns that supported white statues of men on some sort of mounts. Bright green silk draped the reception counter, spilling from it in pleated waves.

She had never seen so much opulence in her entire life.

Ven strode to the reception area across the polished floor inlaid with a green and gold mosaic. A man with a practiced smile greeted him.

"Venturo Escana to see Savien Sangori," Ven said. "I'll show myself up."

Heads turned. Suddenly they were the focus of attention.

She felt the sharp points of psycher minds approaching from the left, where a gilded elevator slowly descended along the wall. Ven had felt them too, and moved to stand in front of her.

The elevator doors opened and Castilla de Solis walked out onto the floor. Her mind blazed like a luminescent supernova. In a split second, Claire assessed it. Castilla had power. The question was, did she have the skill to go along with it?

Behind her two men stepped out, one tall, older, with a square jaw, a walking brick. His mind glowed, not as bright as Castilla's, but strong enough. The man on his left was a leaner, faster, younger version of him, his blue-black hair falling in a long waterfall down his shoulders. His mind rivaled Castilla's, but there was an odd brittle edge to it.

"Venturo," Castilla's eyes opened wide in mock surprise.

"Did you enjoy yourself?" Scorn dripped from Venturo's voice.

The lean psycher's gaze met Claire's. The irises of his eyes were so light, they nearly glowed.

"Yes. Yes, I did."

"Was it worth starting a war?"

"Are we at war, Venturo?" Castilla raised her eyebrows.

"We are now."

"Then I'll start with your pretty little drone."

The lean psycher's mind caught Claire's in a fiery hot grip. Her body locked, her spine bending in an unnatural angle. Her throat constricted, cutting the oxygen flow to a mere trickle, letting in just enough air to retain consciousness. She began to dismantle the shell from within.

The lean psycher's eyes widened, puzzled.

"She isn't screaming." Castilla blinked, feigning surprise. "Do you restrain your drone often, Ven? Perhaps she likes it?"

Venturo moved. The force of his mind shot out like a blow of an enormous club. The older man went flying across the lobby, his heavy body knocking the golden chairs into the air. Venturo spun, too fast, and then Castilla was locked in the cage of his arms, her back to his chest, his hand holding a red monomolecule blade a millimeter away from her jugular.

"Attacking a civilian is a new low for you," he said, his voice calm, almost conversational. "Shall I tell your parents about it?"

She trembled, rage shivering in the curl of her upper lip. "Kill him!"

The older man slowly picked himself up off the floor. His nose, mouth, and eyes bled. The lean psycher stared at Ven.

"Kill him!"

"They can't, dear," Ven told her, his lips a few centimeters from her ear. "You can't fight me with your mind. We've tried that, remember? If your cousins attack me, they'll have to spend time breaking through my outer shield. My blade will end your life in half a second. And then I'll kill both of them, and if I don't, your father will."

Castilla growled, a purely animal sound suffused with helpless fury.

"So sweet and refined," Ven said. "As always, a true blossom of the Provinces."

"Fuck you!"

"Perhaps later, if I decide to go slumming." Ven nodded at the lean psycher. "Pelori, let her go. Now."

The hold on Claire's mind vanished. Her heels touched the ground. "Thank you," she said to Ven. "Shall I alert the authorities?"

"There is no need. We're finished here." Ven let go of Castilla and the woman shoved away from him.

"You'll regret this," she snarled.

"I had to touch you - I'm regretting it already."

Castilla spun and walked out of the lobby. The older man followed. The lean psycher lingered, looking her over, and walked away.

"Are you alright?" Ven asked, his mind probing hers gently, searching for damage.

"I'm fine." She forced calm to flow through her outer thoughts. "Shall we go up?"

"No. I've changed my mind." He leaned closer and murmured, "We won't get to Sangori now. He's had too much time to prepare." He raised his voice. "Will you join me for dinner instead?"

"Of course."

"Excellent."

They walked out. The moment they boarded Venturo's sleek silver aerial, the force of his mind flowed over hers, like a shield. "Will you let me scan your mind for injuries?"

"I would rather not."

"Why?"

"We're not that close," she told him. "I like to keep my thoughts private. I ask you to respect this boundary."

"Very well." Ven punched the code into the aerial's console, pulling his mind back. "Where would you like to eat?"

Claire considered it. She could tell him to take her home. In all likelihood, he simply wanted to observe her to see if her mind unraveled. But he was right here, next to her, and he was offering her an evening of his undivided attention. It wasn't in her power to turn it down.

I'm so pathetic.

If she was going to do this, she would make the best of it.

"Somewhere private," she said. "I think I've had enough excitement for today."

The aerial's engine hummed as they rose into the air. "I know just the place," he said.

Claire had no idea that the top floors of the Guardian Building housed a garden. In this part of the structure the outer exoskeleton of plasti-steel beams sloped, forming the upper curve of the flower bud, and the space between the diagrid and the inner core of the building was only about twenty-five meters. Those twenty-five meters were occupied by a tiled deck. Ornamental shrubs and flowers formed green barriers, slicing the deck into small private sections. Ven brought her to the larger of these sections.

Three comfortable wicker chairs with burgundy-red cushions waited in the center of the deck, each with its own side table, arranged around a large metal brazier. Past the chairs, the solar panels of the sloping diagrid had turned transparent, reacting to encroaching darkness. The sky spread before her, vast, endless, tinted with purple and blue, the stars distant points of light. Little white flowers bloomed in the flower beds, filling the air with a refined perfume reminiscent of peaches.

Venturo took an ornate bin from behind one of the chairs, dumped a small heap of uniform black stones out of it into the brazier and added wood chips.

"What's this?"

"Charcoal."

"Fossil fuels? Really?" How quaint.

"It's a provincial tradition." He drenched the coals in some fluid and lit it with a flick of a spark stick. The coals ignited. A wave of heat washed over Claire. She smelled smoke. It wasn't an unpleasant scent.

To their right, the glass doors opened and a smiling man came forward, followed by a computerized trolley.

"Ah. Here comes our food. Thank you, Ertez."

"You're welcome. Enjoy."

The man departed. The top of the trolley opened like a flower, revealing half a dozen larger dishes, each supporting long skewers threaded with vegetables and meat.

"Pick one."

She puzzled over the choices and chose a skewer at random. "This one."

Ven lowered the skewer into the openings cut in the rim of the brazier, picked out his own skewer, and placed it next to hers. Flames licked the meat.

"Do you feel lightheaded at all?" he asked casually, plucking a bottle painted with an icy lace of frost from the trolley. "Any strange vision problems, like tiny glowing threads flying about?"

He was trying to check if she'd suffered any mind lesions. Claire smiled. "I'm fine."

Ven opened the bottle and poured shimmering pink liquid into two glasses. "I'm sorry. I should have never put you into that position."

Ven would have never attacked a civilian. In his mind, that sort of action was filed under It's Just Not Done. His mind-shields were down - probably so he could scan her mind at the first sign of trouble - and his emotions leaked out. He was intensely worried about her well-being.

Claire smiled.

"Am I funny?"

"No."

"Then why are you smiling?"

"I find your customs - Dahlia customs - antiquated. Charming, but antiquated."

"We're a very violent society," he said, turning the skewers. "We have to have customs and ceremonies, otherwise we'd constantly offend each other and soon none of us would be left. Some things are not done. Attacking a civilian is one of them."

"Were you worried?" She sipped the pink drink. It was sweet, tart, and refreshing, with a trace of alcohol. She realized it must be wine.

"Yes," Ven said. "I was worried. I didn't want you to be hurt because I was caught off-guard."

"I wasn't worried," she told him.

"I noticed. You handled the whole situation with the poise of a seasoned kinsman." He laughed. "A violent psycher paralyzes your mind, and when he lets you go, you calmly ask if you should alert the authorities. You kill me, Claire."

Kill. A dangerous word. "I considered screaming in blind panic, but I didn't want to break your concentration."

"Was that a joke?"

"Possibly."

He raised his glass. "Congratulations."

"Thank you." She grinned and drank her wine.

Ven frowned. "I don't know what Castilla has on Sangori, but I called a friend of mine in the Provinces, Celino Carvanna. The man is a financial shark, so if something is going on with Sangori, I will soon know about it."

Ven took a plate from the trolley, used a fork to slide the meat and vegetables off the skewer onto it, and passed it to her. Claire took a bite. The meat tasted smoky and tender and completely delicious.

"This is great."

"There is something about food cooked over the open flame," he said. "I don't know if it's a racial memory from the time we huddled around the fire in animal skins, but there are few things as flavorful."

He raised his glass. She raised hers and he clinked it against hers. "Do you like the wine?"

"I love it. This is my first taste."

"No wine on Uley?" he asked.

"No. Occasionally we would be issued grain alcohol, but no wine." She bit the meat and chewed, savoring the taste. "Do you and Castilla have some sort of prior history?"

Ven sighed. "Yes. Yes, we do. My father was an off-worlder. He came to Rada with nothing except the clothes on his back, but he was a very powerful psycher and my mother's family took him in. He became a client. It's the next step up from a retainer. When you're a client, you are almost family. My father fell in love with my mother and she fell in love with him. They married. He took the Escana name, because our family had status and name recognition, while his surname meant nothing. They were both older at the time, so it was a surprise when I came along."

"Were they happy you were born?"

He nodded. "Yes. I had a happy childhood. The money was tight, but tight by kinsmen standards. We had a nice house. During summers, we'd go to the coast to swim in the ocean. It was beautiful. Endless water, brilliant blue as far as you can see and under the surface fish in every color. The mountains thrust right out of the water, and I'd sit on the rocks and watch the shark dolphins play..."

She almost said, "You see the bionet as the ocean, don't you, Ven?" but caught herself. Claire Shannon, the secretary, wouldn't know that.

"My parents loved it so much, they live there now. I always wanted to live on the coast." Ven smiled.

"So why don't you?"

"There are very few businesses on the coast. The ocean storms six months out of the year, so little shipping is done by water. The ports are mostly for tourists. Besides, most of the family is here. Our business interests are here. My father and mother have little concern for Guardian. Neither one of them is really the business type. They have the ability, but not the ambition required to grow a business."

Ven shrugged, leaning back. His face seemed almost melancholic, and then he shook it off.

"Anyway, back to Castilla. As I grew up, the family realized that I was their most valuable asset. I'm a stronger psycher than my father, but we had very few resources to make use of my talents. De Solis is an old family. A lot of money, a lot of connections, and decades in the bionet business. So, my parents approached the de Solis with a marriage proposal. De Solis would get a powerful psycher and Escana's financial issues would be resolved through the alliance."

He seemed unperturbed by the idea of his family selling him. "How did you feel about it?"

Ven drank his wine. "Imagine that you're eighteen years old. On this world eighteen means you are a man, expected to support yourself and your family. You're the golden child; your family expects you to lift them out of misery and solve all their financial problems, and you have no idea how to do that. You have a lot of anxiety about it. Then your father comes to you and says, 'You don't have to go to college and you don't have to worry about finding a job. All you have to do is marry this beautiful girl, make her happy, and work for her family business. They'll train you, they'll teach you to develop your talents, and one day you'll inherit the whole enterprise. You'll never have to worry about a thing.'"

"Sounds great," she said.

"I was all about it," Ven said. "Ask any eighteen-year-old boy and he will tell you he'd jump on the chance. And Castilla was gorgeous. She had breasts the size of grapefruits."

Claire blinked.

"I'm trying to give you my eighteen-year-old perspective."

"So her breasts were a large factor in your calculations?"

"Yes. Sex with a beautiful girl on a regular basis, I wasn't going to pass that up." Ven shook his head with a self-mocking expression.

She laughed.

Ven refilled their glasses.

"What happened?" Claire asked.

"It turns out that I knew about the negotiations, but nobody bothered to tell Castilla. She was sixteen at the time and she was a kinsmen princess: expensive clothes, pricy jewelry, endless parties... Anything daddy's money could buy, she bought. She set the scene. She had a crowd of flunkies following her around, egging her on." Ven stirred the coals with a metal poker and set a few more skewers over the fire. "Somehow the rumors of the possible engagement leaked and one of the tabloids cornered her.

She was at a party at the time, surrounded by her hangers-on. They asked her what she thought about the engagement."

He fell silent.

"What did she say?"

"She said, 'Well, of course every beggar boy wants to marry a princess, but princesses don't dream of marrying into panhandler families.'"

Even with her minimal knowledge of Rada, Claire knew the insult to the Escana family was monumental.

"The tabloid had her on vid, and they ran with it. Her father tried to quash it, but it was too late. The engagement was impossible after that. Castilla's parents were furious with her."

"Because of the insult to you?"

"That, but mostly because her conduct was vulgar. It made her seem stupid and spoiled and it was unbecoming of her family name. Kinsmen mothers would play the vid for their children as a demonstration of how not to behave in public. De Solis had been above reproach and now they were deeply shamed. Her father told her, 'You think you're a princess? Let's see how you will do without my money.' Everything stopped, all her parties, all her shopping sprees, all of it went away. Her crowd dumped her. She worked for the family company and was given just enough money to live on. To this day her spending is tightly controlled. She hates me. You saw her today, she was practically frothing at the mouth."

"You hate her, too."

Venturo stirred the coals again, the light of the fire playing on his face. "It took me eight years to scrape together enough funds to start Guardian. I took every job I could find. I remember two months after Guardian opened, a contract fell through. We couldn't pay the power bill. We got one terminal working, because we had to log in and patrol for our monthly maintenance. We had it running off the aerial's generator. I'd drained it dead. When I think where I could've been if we had married... She set me back about fifteen years."

Fourteen years ago the Intelligence soldiers had led her away from her mother's apartment.

"Do you regret it?" Claire asked.

"No. If I went down that road, I wouldn't be the person I am today. I'm not indebted to anyone. I own my business, I own this building, many people feed their families because I provide them with jobs. I got there on my own. Nobody tells me what to do."

"Except Lienne."

Ven grinned. "Except her. She never lets me forget that I have family obligations. The other day she actually sent a pulse through the building looking for me. It's a kind of psycher wake-up call."

Yes, I know, it gave me a headache. Claire bit her tongue.

"Besides, I'd have to be married to Castilla." He grimaced.

Claire sipped her wine, feeling the pleasant heat slide down her throat. "Why aren't you married, Ven?"

He shrugged. "I work. A lot. Psychers aren't exactly a common kinsman variant and dating non-psychers is difficult." His face slid into a suave expression. "Hello there," he said in a smooth bedroom voice. "My name is Venturo Escana. I can read your mind!"

Claire laughed.

"I can tell when you're lying and I can discover all your secrets. I'll know when you fake it in bed, I'll know when you cheat, I'll know when you spend too much. I'll know what you really think about me. Don't you want to marry me?"

She finished off her glass and squinted at him from above the rim. "Would you read your wife's mind? You don't read our minds at work."

"Probably not," he said. "But there is always the possibility that I could and that's enough. Your turn to tell me about yourself."

"It's not that interesting," she said.

"I'm interested. I'm dying to know how you ended up on that planet."

She sighed. "Very well. Melko and Brodwyn are actually large mining conglomerates. Both of them owned mining fleets and they strip-mined asteroids for years. It takes a lot of skilled workers to run mining operations on that scale. Mining fleets always attract weird people, individuals who don't fit anywhere else, and the employees of both conglomerates had pretty varied histories.

"Then Brodwyn scouts discovered Uley, which is basically a mineral treasure trove covered with a thin layer of rock. The scouts came back but somehow Melko found out about the find. The official Brodwyn version is that one of the scouts was captured and Melko tortured the information out of her, but official versions are usually untrustworthy. The Melko fleet was more mobile at the time, so they wrapped up their operation and landed on Uley, on the Eastern Continent. It took Brodwyn almost three years to untangle themselves from their trade agreements and then they landed on the Western Continent."

"And the arms race began," Ven said.

She nodded. "The resources were severely limited so both Melko and Brodwyn adopted no-waste policies and encouraged population growth to build their armies. There was only one city on each continent and they looked exactly the same: picture a hive of uniform rectangular buildings about a half-kilometer tall. The buildings were so large, each one was like a village run by a Building Association. You would be born, live, work, and die in the same building sometimes."

"It sounds bleak."

"It was. On most worlds when a war breaks out, both sides have access to prior culture, to art, to pre-war luxuries such as gardens, clothes, entertainment. We didn't. Most clothes were standard issue and un-dyed. We had one solid meal a day, usually a meat block and some sort of grain, the rest of the time we had nutrient paste." Claire hesitated, not sure how much to share. "When I was fourteen, I was taken away from my mother."

"What do you mean, taken away?" He refilled her glass and emptied the rest of the wine into his.

"It was decided that I should become a part of the military support staff, so some soldiers came and took me away from my mother. I was given new rooms in a Military building and I had to live there. My father had died years ago, and my mother was sick with Meteor Shower Virus. A lot of mining people get it - it looks like black burn marks on your skin. Nobody knows why it flares up, but the outbreaks will spark and die out on their own. MSV is incurable. It attacks the nervous system and it's a very slow killer. The victim becomes weaker and weaker, until they lose the ability to walk and then fade into death. All you can do is make the person comfortable."

She took a swallow of her wine.

"Normally a child of my age would be working and would be expected to take care of their parent, but I wasn't allowed to do that. The Building Association stepped forward. The Elder, Doreem Nagi, apparently said that nobody in his building would die a slow death alone. The Elder has the legal powers of a magistrate: he can marry people, divorce them, he acts as a civil judge and so when he made that decision, people listened, and the building collectively took care of her. There were about three thousand people assigned to the building, but toward the end with the war and all only about seven hundred residents remained and every day someone watched my mother and made sure that she had food, was clean, and took her pain killers. I owe them a debt I may never get an opportunity to repay."

"I take back my sad story," Ven said. "Yours is worse."

She shrugged. "There isn't much more to tell. I would wake up, go to work, come home, fall asleep. I did this for fourteen years. And then suddenly the war was over. We didn't even know. They told us we were winning until the very end."

She sensed discomfort emanating from him. Her story affected him, but he wasn't sure how to respond without offending her. Mighty Venturo Escana, at a loss for words.

"Well, that part of my life is over. Now I'm here," Claire said. "Drinking pink wine and enjoying good company.

"And eating meat cooked by a barbaric user of fossil fuels," Ven said.

"I love the food here," she confessed. "I don't know what most things are, so I just order at random."

"New Delphi is the culinary capital of the South. Or it claims to be. Truth is, everyone in the Provinces is expected to learn to cook whether we like it or not."

"Oh?"

"Oh yes. In the Provinces, if a woman is a bad cook, people make jokes." He leaned closer. "Mina, Lienne's daughter? Can't cook at all. Everything she makes tastes awful."

Claire smiled. "I'm sure anything I made would be awful as well. Sometimes when I taste food, my mouth feels overwhelmed. This whole planet is overwhelming: the clothes, the colors, the people..."

He leaned toward her. "You're the most disciplined, grounded person I know, Claire. I've never seen anyone hit the ground running the way you did. Nothing rattles you. If you had a psycher mind, you would be something else on the bionet."

She could tell him. He wouldn't betray her. She could...

"I feel at ease with you," he said. "Your mind is so calm. Every day I deal with people whose minds are a source of constant noise. When we work together, I can finally relax."

She almost screamed in frustration.

"You understand the way I think. I want you to know that I value that greatly. I promise, I won't put you into harm's way again. It took courage to handle it the way you've done. You stood by me. Not many employees would in your place. I won't ever forget that."

Employee... That's what she was, an employee. She shouldn't have deluded herself.

"Did I say something unpleasant?" he asked.

"Not at all. I just realized it's late. I should be getting home." He would never see her as anything else. She was Claire with a quiet mind. That was her value to him. She had mistaken his friendliness and concern for something deeper.

"I'll walk you to the ground floor."

She rose. "It's alright. I know the way."

Ven got up. "Let me walk you down."

She turned and looked at him, keeping her voice flat. "It's not necessary. Thank you for the meal."

Claire turned and walked away.

Chapter Five

"One blue pepper, cut into strips," the Artificial Intelligence announced.

Claire surveyed the small heap of ingredients on her kitchen island. "Define blue pepper."

"Blue pepper: pungent fruit of a Moloccy species rich in lycopene and Vitamin C. Flavor: sweet, slightly bitter. Appearance: dark blue, cylindrical shape tapering toward the tip."

The picture of a blue pepper ignited on the kitchen's digital screen. Claire plucked the pepper from the bunch and placed it on her cutting board. "Demonstrate."

The AI opened a frame showing a woman deftly chopping the pepper into five millimeter wide rings.

Claire watched it for a few seconds, picked up the knife, and chopped the pepper.

It was Saturday morning and she had woken up with a sudden need to prove to herself that she could cook. Immigration had fully stocked her refrigerator with raw ingredients, so she set them out on the counter and had the AI run a comprehensive analysis finding a combination that would result in a beginner-level recipe.

"One peeled compa, cut into strips."

"Define compa."

"Compa: fleshy fruit of Karlovskaya species, rich in Vitamin A. Flavor: sour, with sweet aftertaste. Appearance: red tetrahedron with rounded corners."

Claire picked out a rough pyramid-looking red fruit. "Demonstrate peeling."

The woman on the screen scraped the compa with some sort of implement that did not look like a knife. Claire pulled open the kitchen drawers, rummaging through until she found a similar looking tool.

A soft chime rang through her apartment.

"You have visitors," the AI announced dutifully.

Venturo. Her heart hammered. Her mouth went dry.

"Visual," she said.

The screen ignited. Claire's heart sank. Tonya stood at the door, accompanied by an old man and another that looked in his early forties.

She clenched her teeth, furious with herself. This obsession with Ven had to end. It was turning her into a nervous wreck, catapulting her from one emotional extreme to the next. Enough was enough. Claire exhaled, finding calm.

"Open," she said.

The door swung open, and Tonya and the man in his forties bowed, letting the older one through the door first. Claire wiped her hands on the kitchen towel and walked up to greet them.

The older man examined her, taking her measure. Age whitened his hair, and he walked leaning on a cane, but the eyes that looked at her from under the thick eyebrows remained sharp. He was carrying a satchel. The other man hovered protectively over him. She didn't recognize either of them.

Tonya approached. "Retainer Shannon, we are sorry to call on you so early in the morning, but our need is great. This is Doreem Nagi, our Building Elder, and Charles Monn."

Claire inclined her head, touching her forehead in a sign of respect. "Thank you for looking after my mother."

Doreem nodded to her.

"We seek your help," Tonya said.

"Please sit down." Claire led them to the couches. Everyone took a seat.

Charles reached into his shirt and pulled out a small tablet. On it an image of a blond teenage boy glowed. The boy's face wore the familiar Uley expression: a flat mask, betraying nothing.

"This is Edu," Charles said. "He's fourteen."

The image slid, turning into a portrait of a teenage girl. "Lada."

Another image, another child. "Karim."

"They are children from our building, refugees like us," Tonya said.

"They got into a fight at school," Charles said. "With some local kids. One of the local boys involved claimed that his dagger was stolen in the commotion. The dagger was found on the boy's desk the next day with a broken blade. The dagger is a family heirloom. The school is willing to overlook the fight, but the child's family is upset."

"The security forces took the dagger," Tonya added. "For trace testing."

"The children were questioned," Charles said. "None of the three is admitting to theft and neither are they denying it. They aren't speaking to authorities."

It was a familiar tactic: when in trouble, say nothing. "I see."

"If traces of their DNA are found on the dagger, they will be charged with theft and destruction of property. The charge violates their probation. The children will be taken from their families and deported," Charles said.

"Did they steal the dagger?" Claire asked.

"Yes," Doreem said. "Edu took it to punish the other child. Edu is my grandson. Karim and Lada helped."

"I see."

"We've offered to make reparation to the boy's family," Charles said. "In exchange for dropping the inquest. They declined."

"We ask you to..." Tonya fell silent and glanced at Charles. They looked at their hands, uncomfortable.

"We need your help," he said. "The results of the testing must be negative."

"You want me to log into the bionet and alter the trace analysis?"

"Yes." Tonya exhaled.

Claire leaned back. The Security Forces Database would be under a layered protection protocol of at least level three or higher. Cutting into it would be a nightmare.

"You are asking me to break into a security installation. It will be very well protected. There are defenses to be overcome. The precise manipulation of data will require time. It's a lot harder to alter data than to erase it."

"We've collected credits," Charles said. "From the families. We will gladly pay -"

He saw the look on her face and clamped his mouth shut.

"We have insulted you," Doreem said. His sharp eyes stabbed at her. "We ask forgiveness."

"Apologies," Charles bowed his head.

They thought that because she had left the building, she wouldn't understand. They thought she only cared about money. She understood. Every refugee from the building had conspired to save the children. That's what a community did in times of trouble.

"Please continue," Charles asked.

"Think of the data as being guarded by a pack of dogs," Claire said. "The AI defenses. If the pack sees me, they will attack and bark all together, making a lot of noise. This noise will bring men with guns, the actual psychers. To be able to do what you ask me to do, I will need help. I will need decoys that will draw the pack away from me."

"We have people," Charles said. "They are not combat-grade, but they can move through the bionet."

"They are utility repair people." Tonya said. "They used to check the bionet installations for the failing sectors."

Low-level psychers, with a mental talent too slight to be

affected by the PPP. She'd encountered their type on the bionet before: they could move through it but they had never fought on it.

Claire sighed. "If we're discovered, every person involved will be deported. The children may survive. We will not. Melko will murder all of us."

"We understand," Charles said. "I'm one of those who will be going in with you. We can't do anything more than run, but we'll risk ourselves for the children. We will do everything we can to help you. If you choose to do this."

In her mind Claire was back in her mother's apartment, sitting by the bed, holding her mother's hand. The medic had given her less than twenty-four hours, and Intelligence had permitted her this last visitation. She remembered everything in crystal clear detail. The dark spray of black marks on her mother's face. The smile on her mother's lips. Her mother's hair, clean and braided away from her face. Her mother's voice. "I'm content, sweetheart. I'm tired, and it's time to go. Don't cry. I didn't suffer. They say the passing will be peaceful."

Logging into the bionet meant risking everything. Her job. Her life. Other lives she took with her.

The debt had to be repaid. If she succeeded, she would give three children another chance at life. If she failed...

She had to succeed.

"When was the dagger taken for testing?"

"Last night," Charles answered.

"What time last night?"

"At the end of the school day," Tonya said.

"Take the credits you gathered and rent a large hotel room in the largest hotel you can find," she said. "If asked, tell them you are having a meeting to welcome new refugees in the community. If not asked, say nothing. Pick someone who can pass for a native and have them purchase a portable liquid interface hub, Grade Five or higher. We will need the bionet cognizance units as well. If asked why, say that you are planning a game party on the bionet. We will need a medic and we will need protection for our bodies while we're logged in. Don't involve anyone who can't be trusted to stay quiet. This needs to be done tonight, before the lab personnel return to work on Monday."

CLAIRE WALKED down the polished tile of Hotel Aldebaran's sixteenth floor hallway. Charles had chosen well - the three towers of Aldebaran catered to businessmen and families. People strolled back and forth, parents with children heading toward the hotel's pools, tourists going out to explore the city. Nobody paid her any mind.

She approached the door marked 1672 and rapped her knuckles on the plasti-steel. It swung open and Charles let her inside. The suite's main room was wide and devoid of furniture. A three-foot tall hub sat in the middle of the room, an ornate metal pedestal in the shape of three nude women, each supporting the container of dark-grey liquid interface with her left hand and fondling herself with the right.

Claire raised her eyebrows.

"It was on sale," Charles said.

Doreem sat in the lone chair in the corner. He nodded to her. To the left of him stood a young man with a strong resemblance to Karim, one of the children in trouble.

"Kosta," Charles said. "He's Karim's brother and one of your team."

Kosta looked barely eighteen.

"This is Zinaida," Charles said, bowing slightly to an older woman with startling blue eyes. She nodded back.

"Nonna." A young nervous woman with pale brown hair.

"Saim." Charles pointed at a thin dark-skinned man in his early twenties.

"Mittali." A young woman with very dark hair and light olive skin.

"This is our medic." A blond man in his mid-thirties raised his hand from the portable medi-bot. "Tonya will be assisting him."

Tonya inclined her head.

"Thomas, Sergei, and Helen will watch over us while we're under."

The two men and a woman raised their hands.

They had brought everything she'd asked for. Claire took the bag off her shoulder, removed her sandals, and sat on the rug before the hub. "Join me."

The five members of her team sat in a circle around the hub.

"How many times have you connected?" she asked.

"Seventeen," Charles said.

"Twenty-two," Zinaida said.

"Eight," Saim said.

"Eight also," Mittali added.

"Four," Nonna said.

"Twice," Kosta said.

"Any connections in a hostile environment?"

No answer. She had expected as much.

"Bionet can be overwhelming," Claire said. "However, our minds do their best to cope by transforming it into a familiar environment. Our mind interprets things for us and you must listen to your instincts. If something gives you a bad feeling, it's likely a trap. If you see a monster, it's likely an AI defense or an enemy psycher. You will see strange things on the bionet. Creatures that grow blades. Plants that shoot lightning. You must remember to trust your instincts. If something feels dangerous, it is. Be afraid and be cautious, and you will survive."

"But how do we fight?" Kosta asked.

"You don't. I will take care of the fighting." Claire smiled gently. "Your mission is different. There are two types of threats on the bionet: passive and active. Passive threats are the AI defenses. They remain dormant until an intruder appears. Active threats are psychers like us, humans who patrol the bionet. They are the greatest danger. You will know them because they may look very frightening or appear out of place. For example, if you perceive the bionet as a grassy plain and you see a medium-size predator running at you, it's likely an AI defense. If you see a bovine the size of a house that's sprouting tentacles and tusks, it's likely a psycher."

Claire paused to make sure she had their attention. "If you see a psycher, do not engage. He will kill you. If you see one, and he gives chase, you must run away as fast as you can and disconnect as soon as you are able. Remember, you can only disconnect within a short distance of the hub. Don't be afraid to lead a psycher to the hub. We will destroy it after the mission. Do you understand?"

Heads nodded.

"It's highly likely that you may see me as something terrifying as well. During the mission, I may change my shape in reaction to threats. Don't be alarmed."

"Will you grow tentacles and tusks?" Saim asked, with a hint of humor in his eyes.

"If I have to. We will be going into a secure sector; however, a security forces laboratory is unlikely to have an active defense. It doesn't contain any of the financial or valuable data hacker psychers usually want, so there is no need for a psycher to actively control it. The laboratory will have passive defenses instead. There are three types. First, the loop traps. These are bionet connections designed to lock a mind into a loop in an effort to keep it from reaching its destination. People typically see these as quick sand, swamps, iced over water, and so on. If you are caught in a loop, do not panic. Clear your mind and imagine yourself escaping. If that doesn't work, picture falling through the trap and landing by the hub. That usually initiates the expelling protocol. You will land by the hub and will have to log off.

"The second type of traps are the damage events. Falling rocks, geysers of molten lava, mud slides, and so on. These are the coded defenses. They will activate when triggered but they have a limited range. If you are caught in one of these, you will take damage. Sometimes severe damage. Your mind may develop lesions or become 'bruised.' You may see something that looks like a glowing worm or a tangle of luminescent threads. Sometimes the world will abruptly darken or become too bright to see the objects. If you experience visual anomalies after a damage event, you must tell me immediately. Remember that your range is shorter than mine. I can broadcast my thoughts from a large distance, which means you will hear me but I may not hear you. If you take damage and I do not respond, you must log off as soon as possible."

She waited for everyone to nod.

"The third type of traps are the chasers. The chasers are the defense entities produced by the AI. They are usually perceived as something alive: dogs, insects, sharks. The chasers will actively pursue you. If a large number of the chasers are destroyed, the AI will sound the perimeter alarm, which will bring a living psycher responsible for the security of the sector on our heads. This is something we want to avoid at all costs."

"Why?" Saim asked. "I mean, can't you just fight him or her off?"

"Right now all of us are guilty of conspiring to alter data. It is a non-violent offense," Claire said. "If we confront a psycher, I may have to kill her. Terminating a human mind of a Rada citizen is a death sentence for everyone in this room."

Sudden silence claimed the room.

Claire was the first to break it. "This is why I need you. Your purpose is to follow me until we encounter chasers. As soon as chasers find us, each of you must engage one of them and lead them away. You must scatter and take them with you to keep the AI from sounding the alarm. You don't have to fight. You just have to run and keep them occupied to let me accomplish my task without having to destroy them. Even if all you do is make circles around the hub, as long as they are following you, I will be able to do everything I need to do."

"How will we know when you're done and it's safe to log off?" Charles asked.

"You will hear a signal. If you don't hear anything or if you become lost, don't worry, I will come and get you. One more thing: don't get bitten. We'll be facing Security Force chasers. Their bite will leave a mark on your mind. Eventually it will dissipate - usually in a few weeks - but until then if you log into the bionet, anyone there with you will instantly know that you've tried to break the law. If you are unsure, now is the time to take a step back."

Nonna swallowed and got up. "I'm sorry. I can't. I just can't."

"It's alright," Claire told her. "Nobody here will judge you. It's fine."

The young woman backed out of the circle and went into the other room.

"Anyone else?"

Nobody moved.

"We're ready," Charles said.

Claire took a deep breath and began to dismantle the shell over her mind.

Five minutes later the last vestiges of the shell crumbled in her mind. It felt unbelievable. It felt as if she had been carrying a heavy burden, and chained to it for so long, she had forgotten it was there. Now it was gone. Claire felt light, so indescribably light.... Her mind soared like a bird, stretching, touching her team's minds, establishing a link.

The five stared at her.

"Wow," Kosta whispered.

Claire sent a focused thought. "Lay down and try to relax."

"I've heard that before," Mittali murmured.

Saim laughed nervously.

They lay on their backs, their heads toward the hub. Tonya approached, carrying bionet cognizance units, half-bands of ornate, inert plastic, each sealed in its own transparent wrapper. Claire rose and approached Charles. "Are you ready?"

He swallowed. "Yes."

Claire took the first unit, tore the plastic sleeve, and pulled it out. The steel-colored half-band had three holes: a large oval space on the left and two oblong narrow openings on the right. A thin sheet of disposable plastic sheathed the inner side of the unit. Claire peeled it off, revealing adhesive underneath, carefully positioned the unit over the right half of Charles's forehead, just above the eye, and pressed it down. The plastic adhered to the skin. Charles clenched his teeth.

"Relax." Claire dipped her fingers into the basin of liquid interface in the hub. The mix of metal and synthetic neurons nipped at her skin with sharp electric teeth.

"Once you are in, don't move. Wait for me."

She pulled the interface away from the hub. It stretched in spider-thin strands from her hand. Claire touched Charles's skin, letting the interface drip into the first opening of the unit. The dark-grey liquid filled the hole in the plastic, forging connections through the skin. Claire touched the left opening, letting it fill, then the right. Charles blinked. The band ensured that connections were made to the right areas of the brain. The filaments of the interface thickened as more liquid flowed from the hub, reinforcing the connection.

Charles closed his eyes. His body straightened, aligning, and relaxed. He was in.

Claire moved on to Zinaida.

"AM I DOING IT RIGHT?" Tonya murmured.

"You're fine," Claire said, feeling the prickling of the liquid interface as it filled the last opening in the cognizance unit. "Thank you."

She closed her eyes. Darkness flowed over her as the synthetic neurons made connections with her mind. She lunged down a dark circular tunnel, faster and faster. She had done this thousands of times over the years and she knew what awaited her on the other end - sometimes it was a bleak cliff or severe steppe, but in the past two years it had been a dark forest, uniform tree trunks and pale green leaves.

She welcomed it. She yearned for it. She missed the chase, the thrill of the battle, the infinite possibilities the bionet offered. It probably said volumes about the hypocrisy of her morals, but in that moment Claire didn't care.

Light exploded and she landed, falling into a practiced crouch.

The ground under her was intense, shocking green. Bright yellow flowers, their petals thin and long, all but glowed in the silky grass. Claire raised her head.

Jungle breathed at her. Tall grasses with blade-shaped silvery leaves surrounded dark bushes, their foliage splaying out in wide rosettes. A patch of hair-thin stalks tipped by lavender crests of petals thrust through the spaces between wide oyster-shell plants, the inside of their leaves a blinding turquoise. Massive trees, a dozen meters wide, thrust to the sky, spreading their crown so high above, looking at them made her dizzy. Vines dripped from their branches in thick ropes, bearing large blossoms with triangular petals of deepest crimson. Ferns coiled by the thick roots. Emerald green moss cushioned the bark, interrupted by bubbles of some orange-red plants and ridges of lemon-yellow mushrooms.

Claire stared, shocked.

Creatures crouched around her, a pale blue bull with six horns; a gazelle with golden hooves and wide antlers; a fox with three tails, her bright orange fur rippling with flashes of yellow; a flightless bird on two sturdy legs with blue and green plumage; a slick lupine beast with black fur and six legs; and a bearded ape, fast and agile, his chocolate fur stained by rings of beige.

"Oh my god, oh my god, oh my god," the ape whispered and she recognized Kosta's voice.

Behind her the sound of falling water marked the hub: what was once a three-foot-tall metal sculpture turned into a ten-foot-tall stone fountain. Water spilled from the top in clear sheets and fell into a mirrored basin at the feet of the three women.

Claire looked into the basin and saw herself in its depths. A giant panther stared at her. Her fur was blood-red, striped with slashes of silver. Her eyes glowed with brilliant gold. A mane of pale red streamed from the back of her head, flaring around two pairs of long black horns that thrust up and to the sides behind the bright tufts of her ears. Her wide paws bore black claws the size of swords. She flicked her tail and saw it was tipped with a long tuft of pale red fur, hiding a wicked black spike. Claire smiled and saw the sabers of silver fangs in her powerful mouth.

Sensory overload. She had suffered a culture shock after the planetfall. The province of Dahlia bloomed in her mind with all its colors, scents, and flavors and it reshaped the bionet. What once was a grim forest had evolved into a lush jungle.

Claire bowed her head. "Is everyone with me?"

Voices chorused back in agreement.

"We go," she said.

They began their run through the jungle, leaping over the fallen trees and dashing past exotic flowers. She kept the pace brisk, but not tiring. They'd have to save their strength for later.

The path curled and they shot out onto a cliff. Far to the right an enormous tree rose, its branches glowing with bright purple lanterns.

"A castle," Saim-Wolf whispered.

Mittali-Bird laughed. "A spaceport!"

"That's where we're going," Claire said. "Follow closely, and remember the way. You will be retracing your steps on your way back."

They followed the path down the side of the mountain.

Half-way down, a low rumble under her paws told Claire a trap had been set off. She felt the terrestrial shock rush upward, above them.

"Run!"

They dashed left and down, angling away from the slope. Above them enormous rocks shot out, spinning, and chased them down the slope. The boulders slammed into the side of the mountain with loud thuds.

"Faster!"

They galloped ahead of her.

A boulder landed inches from her tail.

Zinaida-Fox stumbled and fell. A rock tumbled from above, threatening to crush her. There was no way to avoid it. Claire lunged, shielding the Fox with her shoulder and snarled. The jungle shook. The blast of sound slammed into the boulder, knocking it aside, but not far enough. It slammed into her. The impact resonated through her powerful frame. Claire turned, scooped Zinaida into her mouth, and ran.

Five seconds later the animals collapsed on the grass on the side of the mountain, while the rocks continued to roll behind them. Claire carefully set Zinaida-Fox onto the ground.

"Thank you," the older woman whispered.

Kosta-Ape rolled on his back and laughed in labored heavy gasps. "Let's do that again!"

"Why are we so tired?" Charles-Bull breathed. "All this, it doesn't exist. We didn't really run..."

"You've forced your brain to make connections at maximum speed," Claire said. "The mind can't do this indefinitely. It becomes fatigued just as your bodies do. Come, we have to keep moving."

They continued through the jungle. Carnivorous plants snapped at their feet. Nooses disguised as vines reached for their necks. Leaves hid pits with spikes. Saim had fallen into a fissure filled with angry bees and Claire had to jump in after him and fry the insects with a focused mental blast.

Finally, scratched, bruised, and tired, they emerged from the jungle to the edge of another cliff, this time much lower. They lay down, hiding in the twilight behind the twisted network of roots clenching the mountain.

Directly in front of them the ground dropped down. Far, far below, silvery waters of an ocean lay placid, tinted light pink and yellow to the left, where a golden globe of the sun set, cushioned in soft clouds. Above the clouds, the cosmos spread, vast and glorious, with bright stars melting into the glow of nebulas and distant galaxies.

To the right, past the gulf of the ocean, another cliff rose, naked rock wall topped by a lush jungle. Twin rivers spilled from the cliff, wrapped in feathery mist. Between them the massive tree waited. The purple lanterns glowed, beckoning her.

Claire squinted. A narrow rock spire, like a finger of basalt about a hundred yards wide at the top, thrust from the water between them and the other cliff. A little to the left of their hiding place, a wide stone bridge led to the spire. On the other side of the spire, a thick rope woven of lianas, sturdy, woody vines, stretched to the other cliff. Thick enough for her to cross, if she used her claws and paid attention.

Kosta-Ape climbed the tree to her left and leaned to her ear. "There are mutants on the small mountain," he said.

She saw them too: lean, muscled beasts with the body of a fast hound and the jaws of a crocodile. One, two, three... seven. On Uley, the warning call to a psycher would occur if three or more were killed. Sometimes it only took two.

They could've used Nonna.

Well, no use regretting what she couldn't fix. She would have to take the chance.

"We should go now," Charles-Bull said. "Remember, we're here to save the children. We do this so they can have a life."

The beasts murmured.

"Thank you," she told them. "Stay safe. Don't fall into the water."

Charles bowed his head to her.

Claire bowed back.

One by one they disappeared into the jungle. She lay by the roots of the tree and waited.

A shrill screech announced Mittali. The bird ran onto the bridge, feathers fluffed out, and shook her butt at the dog beasts. The hounds snarled, showing sharp fangs. Yellow frothy spit bubbled up on their lips. They looked rabid.

The bird shook her feathers. "Come on! Come on!"

A single dog peeled off from the pack and charged after her. Mittali lingered on the bridge for a long moment and dashed away. The creature gave chase.

She watched the three others grab their AI beasts one by one. Kosta was last. He scooted midway up the bridge and bounced up and down, hooting. The three remaining creatures snarled in unison.

Kosta jumped, flipping in mid-air.

Showoff.

A dog padded forward.

Kosta jumped again, oblivious.

The AI hound stalked closer. Closer.

The wicked jaws opened.

Kosta jerked back and the dog's teeth snapped together. Kosta's hand snaked out, quick, and slapped the furry muzzle. He hooted and took off, the enraged AI dog at his heels.

Young fool. Claire smiled into her whiskers and slunk into the jungle.

A narrow path led to the bridge. Claire stepped onto it and padded forward on silent paws. A moment and she emerged onto the bridge. The grey stone seemed ancient, cracked and weathered. It was only a mind trick, indicating old frayed code. She pictured the stone fracturing under her weight and wished she hadn't.

The twin dogs raised their ears.

Falling into the water wasn't an option. She would survive the fall, but it would take her a while to climb back up. Every moment she delayed, her team ran the risk of being bitten. Time was short.

Two hounds. The question was, could they swim?

The AI creatures charged together, furry bodies flexing with coiled muscle.

She waited.

The dogs leaped together, ruby eyes burning with bloodlust.

Claire jumped. She sailed above them, landed, and whipped her tail. It slammed into the hound on the right like a battering ram. The furry body flew into the air with a startled yelp and plummeted down into the water of the ocean below. If she was lucky, it wouldn't die.

The last dog attacked. She sent it over the side with a swipe of her paw and sprinted across the rocky spire. The liana bridge waited. Claire put one foot on it, sinking the claws into the woody vine.

So narrow.

Phantom wind pressed at her, pushing at her, trying to knock her off into the water below. Claire crouched, digging her claws into the knotted lianas. She needed to redistribute her mass to reduce angular acceleration. Her body flowed, obeying her mental command. Two sets of whiskers, wide like four stiff ribbons sprouted from her shoulders, stabilizing her the way a pole stabilized a tightrope walker. She could've sprouted wings, but they would do her no good. Bionet didn't support flying. Even the birds did little more than leap and glide.

Claire ran along the liana bridge, one paw after another, claws over claws. The vines trembled under her weight. The other end of the bridge was affixed to a point slightly higher than the spire. She was crawling across and up. Coming back would be hell.

Just keep moving.

Keep moving.

The cliff was almost there. She stretched her left front paw and touched it. Solid ground. One leap... and she'd plummet down into the ocean.

Claire forced herself to slow down, carefully sliding her weight onto the damp soil of the cliff. One paw, two paws, three... and she landed. The enormous tree rose before her. She sat, studying the lanterns, her ribbons-whiskers snaking out to lick one.

"Search: Alacasto Middle Academy."

The lanterns spun, sliding along the branches, as if riding an invisible carousel. A brightly shaped lantern stopped before her, the lavender flame inside glowing brightly. Claire's whiskers touched it, forging a link.

"Laboratory traces analysis: Romulus Rekanta, 99.9959% match; Edu Nagi, 99.97890% match; Lada Miller, 98.87682% match; Karim Jahar, 96.48991% match."

She reshaped the data. A new set of figures flowed into the lantern: "Edu Nagi, 29.97890% match; Lada Miller, 28.87682% match; Karim Jahar, 16.48991% match."

Wiping the molecular analysis to zero would have set off the red flags, but all people swam in the same genetic pool. Anything below 70% would be marked as inconclusive.

The lantern looked exactly the same. She'd altered the data with a psycher's precision.

Claire spun the lanterns, pulling up searches at random, confusing the access protocol until the children's lantern was safely mixed with the others. Her job was done.

Claire spun and dashed back to the vine bridge. Once again the lianas shuddered under her weight, only this time she was crawling head down. She wished there was another way back.

She was ten meters from the rock spire when she heard the bushes rustle near the base of the stone bridge.

Claire conquered the last few meters and moved onto the solid ground of the spire.

A beast shot out of the jungle and landed midway on the stone bridge. Huge paws hit the ancient stones, each as big as her head and tipped with thick triangular claws, razor sharp and glowing like backlit amber. A bronze beast rose, towering over her by at least a meter. Thick muscle slabbed his monstrous forelegs and colossal chest. His hind quarters dipped lower than his shoulders, his back legs bent slightly and bulging with steel-hard muscle. His fur was bronze, painted with faint rosettes of russet, same as the mane that trailed his spine and slid over his shoulder and down each leg almost to the paws.

The beast opened his giant mouth, snarling, showing her brilliant white fangs. His torso resembled an enormous dog, but his head was almost feline. The jaws looked powerful enough to bite through her bones like they were soft candy.

A psycher. A Grade A psycher.

Damn it all.

The beast roared, whipping his triple tail. The blast of sound hit her and Claire snarled back. Her roar rolled, promising pain and blood.

The beast dipped his head to stare at her. She looked into his eyes and saw the familiar intellect glaring back.

Venturo.

No. No, this couldn't be.

The beast leaped.

Claire ducked left, her instincts taking over. A clawed paw came down a hair from her shoulder and she struck with her talons, slicing the bronze fur. The triple tail whipped around, catching her flank. Pain stung her, followed by a sharp spike of heat. Poison. Nice.

Claire shot to the side, rolling out of the claws' way, and strained. Bloody spray shot out of wounds on her side, expelling the poison with it. She sealed the wound.

The beast turned his head and stalked after her, the huge paws raising tiny puffs of dust from the rocky surface of the spire.

They leaped at once, flying at each other. His claws raked her side in a searing rush of pain. She bit his neck, ripping through the coils of tight muscle, but his flesh was too thick to reach bone and she withdrew.

Venturo's blood burned on her tongue.

She had to make it to the bridge. It was her only chance. She couldn't bring herself to kill him.

Dark blood poured from the wound on Venturo's neck, wetting the bronze fur. He took a precious second to seal the gash.

Claire concentrated. She shuddered and split herself, throwing four copies of herself, three to the right and one to the left. Five identical scarlet cats snarled in unison.

Venturo took a step back.

Her copies rushed him and Claire jumped over him, throwing all her speed into a desperate leap.

The triple tail whipped around her, squeezing her like a noose. He'd seen through the phantoms.

She shot her back whiskers into his ribcage, turning them into hard spears in mid-strike. He snarled in pain and she slapped her own tail to slice at his face, trying to skewer him with the spike. He hurled her back. She flew through the air and smashed into the jutting rock wall. Her ribs cracked. The impact shook her vision into a haze.

Claire jumped to her feet and leaped right, left, jumping like a lunatic rabbit to avoid being hit. Her vision cleared and she saw his gaping maw diving down. Claire slapped his face with her paw, her claws raking four deep gouges on his cheek. The blow knocked him aside. He jerked back and they snarled at each other, face to face.

Fire shot from Venturo's eyes, dashed down his fur, and he stood before her engulfed in flames.

The Element Weaponry. The pinnacle of the psycher bionet training. If she had time, she would have bowed in appreciation.

He advanced toward her, menacing, flames swirling around him. She feigned fear and backed away.

A step.

Another.

She would not get another chance. This was her very last one.

Her hind paw found air. She was to the edge of the spire.

Venturo leaned forward, the fire roaring around him.

If he was fire, she would be ice.

Glacial mist shot from her. Claire charged into the depth of the inferno. His fire licked her ice barrier.

They collided.

Claire let go, emptying every last reserve. Spears of ice shot from her, locking him into blocks of ice. She saw his enraged eyes before the ice swallowed him whole.

Claire ran. She ran like she had never before run in her life, swallowing distance in hungry gulps. She tore through jungle, ignoring branches and thorns tearing at her hide. Her mind fired brisk, calm commands, sending the signals down the established links to her team.

"Disconnect. Mission complete. Disconnect now."

A roar of pure rage shook the jungle. Ven had broken through the ice. A mere five seconds, maybe less. It had to be some sort of a record.

She had no way of knowing if her team had made the hub, so she just kept broadcasting. "Mission complete. Incoming threat. Disconnect."

Her mind shuddered under the strain. Her legs began to cramp. Every breath was a fire exploding in her lungs. Up the mountain, up, up, up.

She whirled at the mountain top and dared a single look back. A fiery glow was making its way through the canopy below. He was close. Claire ran.

The world began to fade. Darkness encroached. She was running too fast.

Venturo's furious growl shook the leaves behind her.

Claire burst into the hub clearing. Charles-Bull ran in a circle around the hub fountain, chased by an AI dog.

"I'm the last!" he cried out.

"Disconnect," she commanded.

The AI beast leaped at her, and she crushed its spine with one impatient snap of her teeth.

The bull vanished, exploding into dark ribbons.

Venturo shot into the clearing.

She let go of the bionet, hurling up the tunnel into the hotel room. A long shuddering moan ripped from her lips, and Claire took her first breath.

The reality of the hotel room slammed into her. She sat up and pulled the unit off her head.

Mittali lay on her back next to her, wincing as Tonya rubbed her feet. Charles was breathing hard, as if he'd carried a sack of rocks up a mountain. Zinaida smiled at her. Saim waved. In the corner Kosta sat in a clump, dark head hung down.

Everyone got out alive.

The medic stood by the hub, a glass vial in his hand. Acid, she guessed. "Dump it."

The medic poured the acid into the liquid interface. The liquid hissed as synthetic neurons boiled into nothing.

"Are you alright, Kosta?" she asked him.

"He got careless," Saim said. "He was bitten."

"May I?"

Kosta nodded.

Claire swept over his mind. The lesion was small, but his mind glowed with the imprint of the AI's teeth.

"It will be alright," she said. "Just stay off the bionet for about a month."

He nodded.

"I saw him," Charles said, his voice filled with wonder. "I saw him. Was that a psycher?"

"Yes," she told him.

"It's a miracle we're alive," he said. "You are that miracle."

She shook her head. "You've had no experience and no weapons. You've made it possible."

"We should drink," Saim said.

"Yes. Yes, that's a great idea," Mittali rolled to her feet. "Ow. As soon as I can walk."

"Don't worry," Saim told her. "Tell me what you want, and I'll bring it to you."

Doreem Nagi rose off his chair and walked over to Claire.

"It is done," she told him softly. "Your grandson should be safe."

The old man bowed to her.

Chapter Six

Claire walked down the hallway toward Venturo's office. The shell over her mind was paper-thin. Accreting it took time, and she had barely had thirty-six hours to recuperate.

Saturday night, after she'd returned to her apartment, she pulled the ingredients out of the refrigerator and continued her aborted cooking attempt, convinced that any moment Security Forces led by Venturo Escana would barge through her door. She'd finished the Dahlia Three-Color Stir-Fry and ate it. It wasn't as good as she had hoped, but it wasn't at all bad. Considering the bland food on which she grew up, her taste buds probably needed a lot of education to fine tune her palate. Or perhaps the anxiety that made her jump at every stray noise interfered with her ability to enjoy the meal.

Claire had taken a long, luxurious bath and, exhausted, fell asleep in the bathtub. She dreamed of Venturo, of his green eyes, of his bronze skin, of wanting to kiss him. Her dream-addled imagination conjured the taste of his mouth, the feel of his hands on her body as he stroked her, the weight of his muscular body pressing on top of her. She awoke to a cold bath.

He was as powerful as she had expected and more. When she

thought about their fight, the tiny hairs on the back of her neck stood up.

When she finally crawled into bed, she realized that she had gotten away with it.

He would never find out who she truly was. She curled into a tight ball and lay there for hours, her thoughts too loud, the phantom images of Venturo sliding back and forth across her memory.

Now it was Monday. She was once again the calm, collected Claire. She walked to her office, a comfortable nook on the side of Venturo's glass cage. Today the glass was opaque, frosted with white by a privacy switch. Ven didn't want to be disturbed. Just as well.

She barely had a chance to put down her bag when Lienne approached the office, marching down the hallway.

The older woman nodded at her. "Claire, about the Berruto analysis. I know it was last minute, so if you want to take a few days, it will be fine."

Claire flicked the stylus across the digital screen projected onto her desk and smiled. "It's in your inbox."

Lienne glanced at her tablet. "So it is. Thank you."

"You're welcome."

The older woman regarded her for a long second and rapped her knuckles on the opaque door. The frost melted from the glass. Ven sat inside. He was wearing a bionet suit. Dark circles clutched at his eyes.

Claire forced herself to sit down at her desk and look busy.

Lienne stepped inside the office and crossed her arms. Her mind sent a focused thought.

"Rolando said you and Claire had an intimate dinner in the Roof Garden on Friday."

Ven grimaced. "Rolando needs to keep his mouth shut."

"I've warned you about this, Ven."

His face looked grim.

"I'd gone to see Sangori. Claire insisted on coming with me, because apparently I 'shouldn't go alone.'"

"You shouldn't have."

"I ran into Castilla, Lim, and Pelori. Pelori locked Claire in front of a lobby full of witnesses. She didn't scream. Didn't panic. When I forced him to let go, she landed on her feet and asked if she should alert the authorities. No shaking in the voice. Nothing. She made us look strong and competent. She singlehandedly restored my standing in the community and she doesn't even realize it."

"I know all that." Lienne waved her hand. "The story is making the rounds."

Ven looked up and his eyes betrayed anger. "Then why in the world are you badgering me about serving her dinner? Should I have sent her home and then been notified that her mind developed a lesion and her brains leaked out of her ears?"

Lienne leaned forward, resting her knuckles on his desk. "That's not what that dinner was and you know it. You cooked for her, Ven. You served her pink wine. You were up there for two hours. The only thing missing from this romantic rendezvous were the passion cones and only because the kitchen didn't have any."

Ven leaned back in his chair and sighed.

"There are things that aren't appropriate between the owner of a business and an employee."

"Don't lecture me," he warned.

"I will lecture you. Has it crossed your mind that she may feel obligated to accept your advances?"

"What advances? Nothing happened."

"She can't decline your invitations. In her mind, you're putting her into a position where she must accept your overtures or risk being sent back to a hellish planet where she might be put to death on arrival. You're putting her into a very difficult position."

He waved his hand at her. "Nothing. Happened. It wasn't that kind of dinner."

"Oh? What did you talk about?"

"Nothing. She asked about Castilla and then I asked her about her childhood."

"Venturo! Do you not see the writing on the wall? She is a talented girl, smart, efficient, and conscientious. If you keep pushing this, she may quit to escape. Do you have any idea how difficult it is to find an admin who can actually tolerate you, Ven?"

He stared at her, incredulous. "You didn't even want to hire her! I hired her."

"However she came to work here, she is here now, she is doing exceptionally well, and I don't cherish the prospect of having to replace her."

Venturo raised his hand. "Enough."

"It's not fair to her, it's not -"

"I said, enough!"

The force of Ven's mind tore out. Lienne fell silent.

They looked at each other.

"Why are you wearing a biosuit at this hour?" she asked.

He rubbed his face.

Lienne checked her tablet. "The log says you've been logged into the bionet for the last thirty-five hours."

"I've met a psycher," he said. "Young. Female. Grade A."

"And?"

"She was powerful."

"How powerful?"

Ven met her gaze. "She iced me."

"Don't be ridiculous. Nobody has been able to ice you since you were sixteen years old..."

He just looked at her.

Lienne fell silent. "For how long?" she asked finally.

"Six seconds."

Lienne dropped into a chair.

"Was she DDS?"

He shook his head. "She iced me and took off. I traced her to a portable hub and the connection went dead."

"You have to find her, Ven. If DDS gets a hold of a psycher who can ice you, Castilla will kill you."

"Yes, who would you berate then?" He grimaced.

"Don't be ridiculous," Lienne's tone was soft. "Find her."

"I will."

Lienne rose. "And Ven..."

"What?"

"About our previous conversation: there are ways to go about these things. Your mother knew this and so did your father."

Venturo blinked.

"It's a bit extreme, but who will tell you no?" Lienne shrugged and left the office.

Claire kept her gaze firmly on her desk. Lienne's worries were misplaced. She could've told her that. The end of the conversation made no sense at all.

Ven stepped out of the office. "Claire?"

"Yes?" She forced a smile.

"Clear my schedule for the rest of the week. Split my shift between Victorio, Rukah, and Daneb. I'm not available for anyone for anything unless it's an emergency."

"I'll take care of it."

He nodded, looked like he was going to say something else, and returned to his office instead.

CLAIRE SIPPED HER TEA. It was Friday, and she sat in a soft blue chair of the fourteenth floor recreation room. The room, shaped like a horseshoe, was positioned so the straight wall faced the diagrid. The wall was glass and sometimes Claire stood next to it, looking down the long sheer drop to the lobby. She liked to watch people, knowing that she was all but invisible.

Today she just wanted solitude. She'd dimmed the glass wall to near darkness, shutting off the bright light of the afternoon streaming in through the solar panels of the diagrid until only the pale purple and blue mood lighting remained. Her head hummed. Being a replacement Venturo Escana was a tiring business.

Claire took another sip of tea and checked the tab. Passion raspberry. Hmm. Delicious.

It was thirty minutes past five. The building was mostly empty. The support personnel had gone home, eager to escape and start their weekend, with the exception of the psycher assistance unit. Both Rukah and Angelia were logged in, although Rukah was coming to the end of his shift and Angelia was just beginning hers.

In the past week Claire had made more executive decisions than she cared to admit. Venturo spent every waking hour logged into the bionet. Attempting to reach him proved futile. He simply brushed her off. Lienne carried her own workload and the couple of times Claire consulted her, the older woman defaulted to "Ask Venturo."

In the end she resolved most of the problems herself, under the banner of Ven's authority. If Lienne or he ever realized who had handled most of the arising problems, she would be fired on the spot for overstepping. Claire smiled to herself. Right now getting fired didn't seem overly tragic. Sure, she would have to find a new job, and her probation period had shrunk to a mere six weeks instead of twelve, but it might be worth it.

It would be worth it to be free of Ven. To be free of the fantasy that would never come to pass. She was too proud to spend the entirety of her life as his silent shadow, while he imagined her beating off the prospective assassins with her tablet.

Ven's mind approached.

Claire sipped her tea.

He emerged from the shadowy hallway, the bionet suit adhering to him like a second skin. She ogled him quietly, looking through her eyelashes while pretending to drink from her cup.

Ven dropped a stack of pseudo paper next to her and landed on the couch. "I found you."

She almost panicked, but her shell was firmly in place and thick enough to withstand a probe. "I wasn't hiding."

"Yes, you were. Lights are off, your desk is organized, as if you've left. If it wasn't for your bag, I wouldn't know you were in the building."

"My desk is always organized."

He looked exhausted. The laugh lines around his eyes seemed more pronounced. His cheeks were withdrawn. And yet he radiated a kind of magnetic sexual energy that made her watch him. Being in his presence was like having sex without ever approaching orgasm - she could watch and imagine, but he would never be hers and he would never want her the way she wanted him.

He sprawled on the couch, resting his head on the padded arm rest, straightened his legs, and winced. Cramped. Clocking nearly eighty hours in the bionet in one week will do that to you. She'd done it before and it was unpleasant.

Ven nodded at the pseudopaper. "I found these."

Claire glanced at the sheets. The Quattrone Family quote.

"I know Lienne didn't approve this. Nor did she compile the data for the quote."

She didn't feel like lying. "How?"

"Lienne has a best friend, Fotina Heleni. When they were both sixteen, Deo Quattrone stood her up. They were at a party together, and he saw his ex-girlfriend in the crowd with another kid and made a giant scene. It got ugly. Lienne despises him and the whole family. If her hate were a plasma converter, she could launch a thousand spaceships into orbit."

Claire laughed. "Are you trying to hint that your aunt holds grudges?"

"I'm not hinting. I am saying it. So who helped you with these?"

She sighed. "Would it be so terrible if I had done them myself?"

"The quote shows a detailed knowledge of the bionet," he said. "Who is the co-conspirator, Claire? I promise I won't punish anyone. In fact, I may give this person a raise and unload the rest of the quotes on them. Although that would be a punishment in itself, I suppose."

Frustration boiled up in her. "You're right, Ven. A drone like me couldn't possibly understand the expense involved in structuring the spiral cell protection."

He focused on her. "You are not a drone. We've discussed that."

"And you never like to repeat yourself." She had to stop talking.

Ven sat up, propping himself on the armrest. "Why are you upset with me?"

Say nothing. Say nothing. Claire forced her voice to sound even. "I am not upset. I'm just tired."

"I get it," he said. "Unloading all of my work on your shoulders wasn't fair. But I have no choice. You can keep your helper a secret, if you wish. I'll find out eventually anyway."

No, you won't. You can't find someone who doesn't exist.

"You're still looking for your mystery woman?" she asked.

He nodded.

I'm sitting right here. "What's so important about her?"

He sat up. "Have you ever seen a silver shark?"

"No."

Ven reached for her tablet and pulled up the console. His fingers flew over the keys. A large digital screen ignited in the opposite wall. It was intense, deep blue, suffused with rays of pale green light, and she realized she was looking at the depths of the ocean.

Something stirred far in the distance. A hint of movement shifted the water.

A pale silver star winked in the distance.

Another ignited close by it.

Claire leaned forward.

More stars ignited and shimmered with nacre fire, shifting through the entire rainbow spectrum. A serpentine shape swam to her, graceful, beautiful, sheathed with silver scales and rippling with color. The sleek creature paused in front of the camera and coiled, displaying a multitude of wide fins bristling with spikes. There was something hypnotic in the way its body moved, sliding its coils through the water.

"This is what she was...?" Claire asked.

"Yes. It's a silver shark serpent off the Coral Coast. Except she was more like this." Venturo tapped the tablet.

The sea serpent grew, swelling, filling the screen. Her head sprouted ivory horns, tinted with intense electric azure. A mane of silver and blue sheathed her spine, flaring around her head. Some of her fins widened, turning into razor-sharp blades, others grew into wide wheels, rippling with iridescent rainbows. A line of pale blue lights ignited along the serpent's body. She gathered herself.

The lights pulsed.

Sharp blades of ice exploded from the creature, freezing the screen.

That's how he saw her... "How did you get this image?" Claire said, her voice barely above whisper.

"I drew it with imagining software," he said. "From memory. It doesn't do her justice. She was incredible. I wish you could've seen her, Claire."

The admiration vibrated in his voice and suddenly she was intensely jealous of herself.

"I've never seen anyone like her," Ven said. "Every psycher sees the bionet in his own way. I see it as a shallow ocean with islands. I was patrolling when I got a ping from one of the Security Forces installations."

"I didn't know Guardian had any Security Force contracts."

"It's not a fact they want us to advertise," he said. "Anyway, I swam that way and saw her. She had accessed a coral tree - the installation's data banks - and was coming back. She had to slither down a spike-studded channel barely wide enough to hold her. Thirty centimeters in either direction and she would've been skewered. It was insane."

He sounded obsessed.

"How do you even know it was a woman?" Claire murmured.

"A feeling I got. I brushed past her mind and it seemed familiar somehow. I've met her before. I've been breaking my brain trying to recall where and nothing." He rubbed his face.

She couldn't help herself. "Maybe she came to apply for a job."

"No. I would've remembered."

Oh, you idiot.

"And I would've hired her." Ven sighed.

Claire set her now empty teacup on the table. "Just out of pure academic curiosity, what are you planning to do if you find her?"

"I'll drop to my knees and propose marriage on the spot."

What?

He leaned back and laughed. "You should've seen your face. I finally managed to rattle the imperturbable Claire Shannon."

She almost hit him. "All this time in the bionet has clearly altered your thinking patterns."

"If I see her, I'll try to buy her," he said. "Or kill her. I haven't decided."

"That's a bit extreme."

"If DDS finds her, they will do the same," he said. "Not only is she a Grade A psycher, she's been trained. She has the kind of combat expertise that takes years to master. During our fight, she cloned herself. She actually made copies of herself and they moved independently of her. They lasted only a second or two, but it would be very useful in a fight. I've been trying to figure out how she did it."

It's not that difficult, really. You shed copies of your outer thoughts within milliseconds of each other. Same process that produces your shadow. Claire clamped down on that thought before it turned into words.

"Well, good luck in your quest," she said. "I think I'll go home now. I've spent too much time in this building this week."

"That's an excellent idea." He rolled off the couch and stood next to her. He was half a foot taller and he was standing too close. If she raised her hand, she could touch his face. "Come on a trip with me."

What? "Where?" she asked calmly.

"To the provinces. I need to see a friend of mine anyway, so we can pretend it's a business trip."

"And what would it be really, if not a business trip?" she asked.

He leaned toward her a fraction of an inch. His eyes laughed. "It would be me and you getting away from this building."

What did that mean, exactly? "Your aunt wouldn't approve," she said.

"I can go whole days without giving a damn about what my aunt thinks. Weeks even. Come with me, Claire. You've never been to the provinces and Celino's wife is a fantastic cook."

She hesitated, still not sure if the offer was genuine or if there was some hidden catch.

"It's not an order," Ven said. "Just an invitation from a friend. Whether you accept it or decline will have no bearing on your position with this company. I don't want you to feel obligated."

"I don't," she said. "How far is it?"

"About an hour by aerial at top speed. I promise to have you home before midnight."

"Why midnight?"

"When you take a young girl out with her parents' permission, it's understood that you must return by midnight." He shook his head. "It's just an expression. Forget it. Come with me."

"Are you sure your friends won't mind my presence?"

"I'm sure," he said.

"I need to get my bag."

"I need to shower. Tenth floor deck in fifteen minutes?"

Fourteen minutes later she climbed into his aerial. Ven grinned at her. He wore civilian clothes: a dark pair of pants and a light grey shirt that molded to his chest and arms. His hair was still wet from the shower and she smelled a faint hint of his soap. She didn't know the name of the scent, but it made her want to kiss him and see if she could taste it.

"I'm glad you decided to join me," he said.

"Me too." She just hoped she wouldn't regret it later.

The aerial shot into the orange light of the afternoon.

Ven pushed the com and typed in the number. A man's face appeared on the screen: masculine, intense, with harsh grey eyes. His hair was almost blue-black. Recognition flooded the man's eyes. He smiled and became a different person - warm, welcoming. "There you are. We expected you earlier."

"I'm on the way to you," Ven said. "Celino, I'm bringing a guest."

"What kind of a guest?" a female voice called off-screen.

"A young female one," Celino said. "She is a co-worker."

"Oh!" the woman off-screen said. "I better make dessert."

CELINO AND IMELDA CARVANNA lived in a beautiful two-story structure with cream walls and a wrap-around balcony shielded by a green roof. Surrounded by orchards and trees, the house drowned in a vast garden, and as Claire walked next to Ven down the twisted path from the aerial landing pad, a sea of dahlias bloomed on both sides of her: peach, orange, yellow, blood-red, deep purple, blue fringed with white, some large, some small, some with wide petals, some with narrow frayed florets, others a mere single ring of petals around a flat disk in the center. It was as if someone had taken a rainbow, put it into a blender, and tossed the result out.

"Anemone," Ven pointed out different varieties. "Waterlily. Ball. Starburst."

"I didn't know you were a botanist," she said.

"I'm not. Growing dahlias is like a national sport. I remember one year a neighbor somehow bred one that was indigo and wouldn't let anyone have any tubers. Almost started a feud. I think someone got stabbed over it."

Claire laughed.

"It's not funny," Ven said, smiling. "Dahlias are serious business."

Celino and Imelda waited for them on the porch of their house. On the ride over Ven had told her most of the details. Celino's family and his had been neighbors. Celino was twelve years older than Ven, forty-five to Ven's thirty-three, and the two of them didn't pay much attention to each other until Celino, who had become a financial shark and accumulated a huge fortune, decided to retire. He required bionet protection for his rather large fortune and business interests, and so he looked up an old neighbor. They soon became close friends.

Looking at Celino Carvanna now, Claire could barely see the traces of the ruthless financial magnate. He seemed perfectly amicable. Charming even.

"This is Claire," Ven said. "She works with me. Claire, this is Celino and that's Meli."

Celino smiled wide and nodded to her. "Welcome!"

"Thank you."

Celino slapped Ven's shoulder. "I have news for you. Come."

They went into the house.

Meli Carvanna smiled at her. She was short, dark-haired, with big breasts and wide hips, and beautiful brown eyes on a tan face. She looked as if she belonged on the porch of this house, in the garden of dahlias, on this planet. This is what the women Ven grew up with looked like, Claire realized. Standing next to her, she felt at once awkward and inadequate. She would never be like this. She shouldn't have come.

"No matter how much time Celino spent in the city, he's still a man of the provinces," Meli said. "Men retire to discuss Important Business, and we women are expected to entertain ourselves by cooking. Since I already finished dinner, I say we revolt and drink wine on the balcony instead."

"Very well."

Claire followed Meli through the house to the balcony, where they sat in the padded chairs, a small table with two glasses and a bottle of wine between them. Meli poured the wine into two glasses. The golden liquid filled the glasses.

"You must excuse them," Meli said. "Knowing Ven, the Sangori problem is driving him up the wall. There is nothing he hates more than being made to look foolish. He detests it. Always did, since he was a child."

"You knew him when you were children?" Claire kept her face carefully neutral.

Meli nodded. "We all grew up in the same area. Ven's cousin dated my youngest brother. Did I say something unpleasant?"

Claire looked at her. She was sure none of her emotions had reflected on her face.

"I'm trained to assess minute facial expressions," Meli said. "Yours was one of distaste."

"Why would one require such a training?" Claire said.

"I'm an assassin," Meli said. "Or I was, rather. For many years. It's considered prudent to rapidly identify emotions in my line of work." She smiled. "It keeps you breathing longer. So why distaste?"

Claire looked at the flowers. "You reminded me that I am an outsider."

"Oh? Where are you from?"

"Uley."

"So how did you and Ven meet?"

"He hired me." Claire closed her mouth, hoping to leave it at that, but the older woman watched her with a rapt expression. Silence stretched.

"It started with the war ending," Claire said. "I worked as a secretary, so I was viewed as a civilian..."

Twenty minutes later, when she was done explaining, Meli smiled. "I'm glad you and Ven found each other. Celino and I married late by kinsmen standards and Ven is almost as old as Celino was when we married…"

Claire looked into her empty wine glass. "I think you might have an incorrect impression. Ven and I are not a couple. I'm his admin."

Meli sipped her wine. "I see. There go my hopes. It's impolite to listen in on a conversation that doesn't concern you."

Claire drew back. Something rustled in the garden below. A small tan hand clasped one of the wooden columns supporting the roof. The second hand joined the first and a child pulled himself up on the balcony rail. He was tan, with Celino's grey eyes and Meli's chocolate brown hair. A streak of dried blood marked his temple and his left forearm sported a long knife cut.

"How did it go?" Meli asked.

The boy raised his face. "I kicked his ass."

"Good. Go wash up. Your father will expect a full account at dinner."

The boy ducked inside.

"Neighbor kid problems," Meli said.

"Yours is a strange culture," Claire said. "Beautiful, vibrant, and passionate, but also savage."

Meli stretched "It's the planet. It heats our blood and makes us do crazy things. Resistance is futile, Claire. It will claim you as its own sooner or later."

The bionet jungle flashed in Claire's mind. "I think it already has."

When Celino and Ven emerged from the study, they moved to the dining room. They had dinner, a delicious parade of perfectly seasoned dishes, during which the ten-year-old Ramiro Carvanna had to describe in excruciating detail every moment of his fight with twelve-year-old Soldano Chellini. The Sangori problem was discussed briefly - the always prosperous family had made a number of costly investments that failed. The firm was teetering on the brink of collapse and the establishment of the bionet servers was Savien's desperate attempt to project an image of thriving success and drum up more business. Celino pounced on the opportunity as if he'd smelled blood in the water. She couldn't quite follow the intricacies of their conversation, but if everything went their way, Carvanna and Escana would own most of Sangori by the quarter's end.

Ven and Carvanna caught up on the latest gossip. Someone married someone else. Someone's sister left the planet. Someone had engineered a short-life, weapon-grade plant virus and nuked the rival's garden with it. Names floated by her. She could've used her training to memorize them, but she didn't bother. What was the point? They were too vivid and too bright, too familiar with each other, and she simply faded into the background.

Later Claire found herself back on the balcony, standing at the rail, watching the last splashes of sunset as the star rolled behind the gardens. Ven came looking for her. At first, she ignored his approaching mind, then she ignored his footsteps, then he leaned on the rail next to her, and she couldn't ignore him any longer.

"Do you like them?" he asked.

"They are very pretty," she said, surveying the flowers.

"I meant Celino and Imelda."

Why did it matter if she liked them? If she said no, what would it change? "They are wonderful hosts."

He leaned closer, searching her face for something. "Did you not like being here? You didn't say more than two words at dinner."

She wanted to grab him and shake him. Why? Why would he bring her here to this little paradise and show her what she could never have? Why introduce her to a perfect woman she could never be? It was cruel. "I'm just a little tired," she said with a small smile.

Ven turned, leaning with his back on the rail. "Was someone rude to you?"

"Not at all. Your friends were perfectly courteous."

"Then what is it?"

"It's nothing, Venturo. I am just a little tired."

He exhaled. "This would be so much easier if you were a psycher."

She pushed from the rail. "Well, I am not." *And even if I was, I would lock you out of my mind.*

His mind reached out, hovering next to her.

"No," she said sharply. Now wasn't the time for mind scans. If he discovered her shell, he would put two and two together. He still didn't know if he wanted to hire or to kill the mysterious psycher. Venturo was proud. If he realized how thoroughly she had tricked him, he would feel extremely foolish. The choice between kill and hire wouldn't be so difficult then. If he fought with her, one of them would not survive. She didn't want to die and she didn't want to hurt him.

Venturo peered at her. "How did you know I wanted to scan your mind?"

She gave him a cold look. "I guessed. You have difficulty taking no for an answer."

"Does this mean you didn't really want to come with me?"

"That's not what I meant."

"Claire, I told you, you didn't have to accept my invitation if you didn't want to."

"I wanted to come," she said.

She could tell by the look on his face that he didn't believe her. "I think it's better I take you home," he said. "After all, I promised to return you to your life at midnight."

He strode back inside the house. She wanted to scream, but venting her frustration in a loud shriek was out of the question, so she clenched her fist and smashed it into the rail.

Chapter Seven

Claire awoke instantly. Someone's mind had brushed against hers. She could still feel the traces of the foreign presence.

Claire rolled out of bed. The owner of the mind waited outside. It wasn't Venturo. His mind felt different. Besides, after their silence-filled flight back to the city, a visit from him was highly unlikely.

She pulled a pair of pants over her underwear and stepped out onto the balcony.

The light-eyed DDS psycher stood on the ground below her windows. His name surfaced from her memory: Pelori.

He tossed back his long hair, jumped, and scrambled up the wall, swinging himself up to crouch on the rail of her balcony. A combat agility implant. Nice.

A thought zinged to her. "*I know you are not what you seem.*"

She'd thought as much. He had touched her mind and sensed the shell.

"Escana doesn't deserve you. He doesn't even know and he is too blind to see it."

Ven would know, but he was too polite to go ruffling through her thoughts. It was a courtesy she treasured.

"Join us. We will give you things. Money. Prestige. Respect. Safety. A better house."

"You're wasting your time," she said aloud.

"Why do you stay with him? What has he done that we can't duplicate?"

"He brings me tea."

"What?"

"When I hit rock bottom and needed help, he gave it to me expecting nothing in return. He takes an interest in me. He cares about my welfare. He is kind to me."

Pelori turned his head, like a bird examining an interesting worm. *"Castilla will give you enough money to buy all the kindness you want."*

"No."

"What if I make you come with me?"

Claire laughed. "If you touch me, I will take your mind apart."

"You don't have the power."

"Try me."

He pondered it for a long moment. He had no way of gauging her power or guessing at how fast she could dismantle the shell.

Pelori dropped off the balcony, landing in an easy crouch. "I will return."

Claire went inside. She was watched. She wasn't sure if he had contacted Castilla or if his visit was an independent effort. Either way, it would end badly.

Her magic dream of a happy life was beginning to unravel at the seams. If she let herself get caught up in mourning the unfairness of it, she would fail to hold it together. The mere possibility of losing everything filled her with fear.

Claire crossed her arms. She had to keep it together. She had to function and she would fight for her dream.

MONDAY CAME TOO FAST. She had arrived at her regular time and sank into work, refusing to permit any distractions, including Ven's mind in the nearby office.

The digital screen in her desk chimed, sending a glowing pulse of pale blue through her screen. She checked the origin. Calena, Building Security. Now what?

She took the call. Calena's face filled the screen. "Claire, there are people here to see you," she said. "They say it's an emergency. They seem agitated."

Calena panned the camera to the side. Tonya, Charles, and Doreem Nagi leaning on a teenager who had to be Edu for support. Her stomach lurched. Something bad had happened. "I'm coming down."

Claire hurried to the elevator, her heels clicking on the transparent floor. A few seconds later the elevator spat her into the lobby. She crossed the tiled space.

Tonya saw her and would've run forward if Charles hadn't caught her. Doreem's face looked grey. Edu stared at her, wide-eyed.

"What happened?"

"They arrested Kosta!" Tonya breathed.

"What?"

"He got a recommendation for a job," Charles said, his face pale. "They looked at his job history and made him log into the bionet. He had no choice."

And the moment he logged in, his mind lit up with an AI's mark.

Her mind slipped into battle calm. "Where is he now?"

"The Security Forces took him away," Tonya said.

He was in physical custody. There was nothing she could do through the bionet or out of it.

"They're going to deport him. Melko will kill him," Tonya moaned.

Melko would definitely kill him.

Doreem Nagi pushed away from his grandson. His knees began to bend. "Please save my grandson..."

She caught him before he knelt. "Don't kneel. Please."

Charles helped him back up.

There was only one solution. "Come with me."

They followed her to the elevator. She brought them to the fifteenth floor and led them to the conference room only a few feet from the hallway leading to Venturo's office. It was the same room she'd sat in six weeks ago, waiting for her interview. The irony.

"Please rest here," Claire told them. "The bathroom is on your left. Wait for me. Don't go anywhere and don't speak to anyone. Refer anyone who asks why you are here to me."

Charles and Edu gently lowered Doreem on the couch. Claire turned and strode down the hallway.

Ven's office walls were transparent. She saw him behind his desk, watching her as she walked.

She had no idea what she would say.

Claire stopped before the door and rapped her knuckles on it. The glass slid aside and she entered the office.

"Sit down," Ven said.

She saw the set line of his jaw. His face was grim, but whether it was anger or determination, she couldn't tell.

"I need help," she said.

He leaned back. "I'm listening."

"A young man from my building on Uley is in trouble."

"How bad?"

"He logged into the bionet where he was bitten by an AI defensive protocol. The protocol belonged to a security forces installation. He has been arrested. If he is deported, he will be killed on arrival to Uley."

"Would they really kill him?" Ven asked.

"Yes. They informed us that anyone who returned to the planet would be terminated." She leaned forward. "He is a child, Ven. Barely eighteen. He has his whole life ahead of him."

"And this is important to you?"

"Yes. His grandfather made sure that my mother didn't die alone in poverty."

Venturo's eyes were still dark. "I can't call to the security forces and demand they let him go. I need a reason. Can you claim that the boy is your relative?"

She was an orphan, and Doreem would do anything to save his grandson. "Yes."

"Then there is a way we can quash the deportation. You would have to become a client of the Escana family."

She blinked.

"As a client, you become an honorary kinsman and can't be deported. Neither can your family. As your patron, I would be expected to make the call to security forces and demand the boy's release." Venturo leaned forward, his arms on the desk. "The relationship between patron and client is complicated. The client serves the patron's family with devotion and loyalty. If the patron gives an order to the client, that order can't be refused, even if it costs the client his life. However, the patron, in turn, is obligated to use his influence and resources to take care of his client and assumes responsibility for the client's actions. Being a client is an honor. You're worth it."

He fell silent.

Claire waited. There was more coming, she could feel it.

"I dreamed about you last night," he said. "When I woke up, I had a moment of clarity. I realized why I've been trying to include you in things I like and hoping you might like them as well. I need to know where we stand. As a client, you can't be fired. You're not really an employee - you receive a stipend from the family. You can't be deported. It would make certain things a lot easier. For example, if you want to reject an invitation from me, you could do so without..."

"Venturo," she said softly.

"Yes?"

"What do I have to do to become a client?"

"You would have to swear an oath linking you to the Escana family. And, of course, there is a mind link."

A wave of ice-cold fear washed over her. "A mind link?"

"Becoming a client requires a demonstration of absolute trust and submission," Ven said. "A sacrifice must be made. If you were a fighter with combat enhancements becoming a member of a warrior family, you would submit to a thorough background check and then you would walk up to your patron, hand him a blade, and allow him to stab you. You would do so without any move to defend yourself. We're psychers. We don't stab and we don't need background checks. We enter your mind and read it like an open book."

He would see. He would see everything.

Claire sat still, paralyzed.

She had to act. Kosta could be loaded on a spaceship by now. He would not betray her. He would trust her to stand by him. She was his officer. She had taken him on that mission. She had a duty to him.

"I understand that it's a huge commitment," Venturo said.

"I want immunity."

"I'm sorry?" His eyes narrowed.

"I want immunity," she repeated, her voice hoarse. "I don't want to be prosecuted for things you may see in my mind."

He grimaced. "In light of your exemplary service, I'm sure we can overlook the occasional theft of tea and cookies from the office. Everyone steals office supplies now and then."

"Venturo!"

He looked at her.

"I want immunity."

Ven growled under his breath. "You drive me crazy, Claire. I take you to the house of my best friend, and you get upset. I offer you the highest honor a kinsman family can bestow on an outsider and you haggle with me like I'm trying to sell you apples at the market. Just what is it you're hiding in your mind?"

"You will find out if you give me immunity."

He stared at her. Silence stretched.

"Fuck it. I have to know now. You have your immunity."

She rose. "Come with me."

He followed her. They almost collided with Lienne, as she opened the door of the office. Perfect.

"Follow me, please," Claire said.

Lienne arched her eyebrows. "What's going on?"

"I have no clue," Ven said. "Just play along."

Claire led them down the hallway to the conference room. Charles and Tonya scrambled up at their approach. Doreem struggled to rise. Claire crouched by him. "Do you want to save your grandson?"

"Yes," the old man breathed.

"Then you must adopt me. Write me into the building roll. Right now."

Charles lifted Doreem to his feet. The Building Manager took his scroll-tablet from his bag and handed it to Tonya. She held it up. Claire knelt. Doreem placed his hand onto Claire's hair. "By the power invested in me by the War Council, I formally adopt Claire Shannon, Rank Captain, birth date of..."

"... Two thousand seven hundred and twenty six standard," Claire murmured.

"... two thousand seven hundred and twenty six standard into Nagi family as witnessed by these five witnesses."

Doreem pulled the stylus out and carefully wrote her name into the Nagi family and passed the tablet to Charles. Charles signed, gave it to Tonya, then the tablet made the rounds to Lienne, Venturo, and finally Edu.

Doreem examined signatures. "So witnessed. Rise, my daughter."

"Thank you." Claire rose and faced Ven. "Kosta is my nephew. Please make the call, patron."

Lienne's eyes widened. "Patron... Patron?"

"I will explain later." Ven took Claire by the hand. "Come on. You four go down to the security forces station to collect the boy."

"Venturo!" Lienne yelled.

"Later." Ven kept a firm grip on her fingers and led her to his office. They stepped inside. He touched his desk. The glass walls turned opaque, and the faint whoosh announced the activation of the sound barrier.

Ven dialed the number on the digital projection on his desk. "Captain Alvarra."

A long moment dripped by.

"Kinsman Escana," a male voice said. "What may I do for you?"

"You've apprehended a boy, Kosta Nagi. He is a nephew of my client, Claire Shannon Nagi."

"My apologies, kinsman. The boy bears our AI mark."

"He was playing on the bionet and stumbled into the wrong sector. I will be happy to pay the fine."

A number ignited in the corner of the screen. Fourteen thousand credits. More than a quarter of her yearly salary.

Venturo flicked a stylus.

"Thank you, kinsman. Shall I deliver the boy to his home address?"

"No need. His grandfather is coming to pick him up. Thank you for your assistance. You have been most helpful."

"My honor, kinsman."

The screen went dark.

So easy. It was so easy for him.

Venturo looked at her. "Feel better?"

"Yes."

"Rank Captain," he said.

"Everyone must have a rank of some sort." Claire desperately wanted to run away. The door was locked. She wouldn't get far in any case. Besides, she had given her word.

"I will initiate the mind link now," he said. "I'll do all of the work. All you have to do is relax."

"Can I have a minute?" She began dismantling the shell from the inside.

"I'm afraid not." His mind enveloped hers, slicing through her surface thoughts.

Venturo's eyes widened. "What is this?"

She put more pressure on the shell.

"Open your mind, Claire."

"I'm trying. It takes time."

"I'm afraid I must insist."

His mind smashed into her shell. It cracked, caught between the pressure of their two minds. He pushed harder. The shell broke. Her mind soared free and she felt him surge through it, finding all of her secrets. He felt the raw grief of her team's death and the pain of the PPP. He saw the bionet, he saw the red cat, he saw himself as the beast on fire. He saw everything. She desperately tried to hide one tiny secret bit of self, the one filled with fantasies of him, with images of both of them, touching, kissing, making love, but he found it in a fraction of a second.

They sat across from each other, her mind glowing, completely revealed. He knew what she had done, why she had done it, and what she had been thinking while why doing it.

His jaw tightened. His mind was like a supernova, churning with anger and surprise.

Venturo rose from behind his desk and walked out.

Chapter Eight

Claire went home. There was nothing else left to do.

She walked into her apartment and sank onto the couch. She felt exhausted, drained, as if nothing of her remained except for a thin shadow.

She should have felt relief. Finally Venturo knew. She wouldn't have to lie anymore. Her position as a client meant she would be safe from deportation. None of it mattered next to the look on his face. He looked betrayed.

She did betray him, his trust, all while she had fantasized about him. She felt small, shamed, and pathetic. She would cry, except she had no tears, so she curled into a ball hugging her knees.

A knock sounded through the door. Claire's mind soared, checking.

Venturo.

She pulled her knees tighter to her. No.

"Open the door, Claire."

No.

"Open the door."

She closed her eyes and willed him to go away.

An image blossomed in her mind: Venturo, nude, golden, his

big body bracing hers. She was shameless and naked. His lips trailed the line of her neck.

Her whole body shivered in excitement, conjuring a physical response to the fantasy.

Claire tried to scrounge up a mental shield.

In her mind, Venturo flipped her, caressing her back, sliding his hands around her to cup her breasts, his fingers teasing her nipples, sending tiny electric shocks through her. A hungry yearning began to build inside her, a kind of emptiness that insisted on being filled. She felt the steel ridges of his stomach against her back and the thick length of his cock against her butt. Her head swam, as if she were drunk on pink wine.

His hard thigh nudged her legs open...

"Stop!"

"Why?" Venturo's thoughts rolled through her mind. *"I'm only showing you what I found in your head."*

"You were never meant to see it."

"Why not? I'm the object of your fantasies. I should be able to see them."

In her mind, Venturo nuzzled her neck, stroking her breasts. The air turned too hot. Every nerve inside her hummed with pleasure. She felt the heat drain down, focusing between her legs, building into a thrilling ache. His right hand grasped her hip, his fingers hot on her skin. He pulled her closer and she felt him between her legs, stopping just short of thrusting into her.

"Stop..."

"You don't tell me you are a psycher. You meet me on the bionet and then you let me look for you for days like a complete idiot. You fantasize about me, but you don't let me know. You're terrible at sharing."

She had survived over eight hundred combat missions, yet she was terrified to open that door.

"Did you touch yourself while you thought of me, Claire?"

In her mind his hand slipped down, over her hip, tracing the sensitive curve of her stomach, down, lower, slipping between her lips. His fingers dipped into her, into the center of the ache, and came away slick with moisture. He flicked his fingertips against the sensitive bud of her clitoris.

Pleasure shot through her. She cried out.

"What's the matter? Am I not doing it right? Open the door and show me."

In her mind, the phantom Venturo leaned to her ear and said a single word. "Coward."

If she didn't let him in, she would regret it for the rest of her life. "Open," she said.

The door slid aside, and he came through, pulling off his shirt as he walked, revealing the bronze skin of his muscled chest. He kicked off his shoes. His pants followed. She just watched, unable to move.

He stepped toward her. His arms caught her, pulling her to him. She saw his green eyes, dark with need, and he kissed her. She tasted him - the slight saltiness and spice - and smelled the exhilarating scent of his sweat mixing with a hint of his cologne.

His tongue slid into her mouth and found hers. Desire swept through her, melting the last remnants of inhibitions. His tongue licked hers, and in her mind, she was picturing him thrusting inside her. Their thoughts tangled in a glowing whirlpool and she saw herself in his mind, golden and beautiful, moaning in pleasure. His pride still stung. He was still hurt she did not tell him. But none of it mattered. He needed her, not just her body, but all of her, her mind, her soul, her love.

"I want you," he said, his voice ragged. "Do you want me?"

"Yes," she whispered. "Yes," her mind sang, "Yes, yes, yes..."

He unzipped her dress, slipped it off her shoulders, and it fell down. His hands eased her out of her bra. Her panties followed. She wound her arms around him. Her fingers touched the hard muscle of his back. She had wanted this for so long. She caressed him, no longer caring about being ashamed. She slipped her hand lower, stroking the smooth skin of his shaft, squeezing, sliding, wanting.

He made a deep male noise and kissed her neck, turning her around. She put her hands against the wall.

He thrust into her, straight into the center of the aching pressure. She gasped, and he kept thrusting, each stroke sending quakes of pleasure through their bodies and their minds. He kept pumping, moving in a steady powerful rhythm. The happy quakes collided inside her, building stronger and stronger, until her muscles contracted and the ache inside her broke into intense shudders of pure bliss. She cried out and sagged against him, supported by his arm around her waist.

"Did you like that?" He grinned, masculine and possessive, and very happy with himself.

"Yes," she told him.

"Good. Now we reenact mine." He picked her up and carried her to the bed.

"THAT WAS A VERY elaborate dream you had," Claire murmured. She lay with her head on Ven's biceps, exhausted, spent, and euphoric.

"I have a creative subconscious."

She smiled.

"What was the deal with the visit to the Carvannas?"

She sighed.

"Out with it," he said.

"Ven, you took me to this garden paradise, which I could never have, and introduced me to a woman who was more than me in every way. She is beautiful, warm, she can cook like a chef, and then the lot of you sat around and discussed people you've known since childhood."

"I wanted you to like each other," he said.

"I like them. It's just... I can't even cook. I mean, I try, but it tastes odd."

He laughed at her.

"I will never be Imelda Carvanna," she said.

"If I wanted someone like Meli, I would have married a long time ago. I want you. My beautiful, lethal, precise ice dragon. One of a kind."

"That's a terrible pet name," she said. "Ice dragon?"

"Silver Shark? Captain Lethal? Slaughter Maiden?"

"Venturo!"

"Seriously, how many hours have you logged in?"

She shrugged. "Eight hundred and forty two combat missions; with training, a little over forty thousand hours."

"I have fifty thousand hours and I've been logging in since I was six. This is kind of embarrassing."

"You logged in because it was fun and you loved it. I logged in because it was my duty to contribute to the war effort. Eight hours, almost every day. There were times when we'd get stuck, and I'd be in for forty hours at a time. I'd wake up with an IV in my arm and have to relearn how to walk." She shivered.

"But do you like it? The bionet?"

She nodded. "It's what I do. It's what I am."

"I'm glad," he said. "I like it, too."

"I had a squad working with me. Grade B and C psychers. That's where the precision comes from - I had to protect them and I couldn't shield all of them at once, so my only choice was to attack and kill with one or two blows before they attacked my guys."

"You didn't hit anything vital on the bridge," he told her quietly.

She sat up and faced him. "I knew in a sheer power contest you would crush me. You are strong, Ven, stronger than me. Less precise, but stronger. I didn't want to hurt you and I didn't want to die. I had only one chance - to run."

She told him about the school and the dagger and the five repair techs.

"And the kid I sprung free today was helping, I'm guessing?" he said.

"Yes. We did the basic DAD - draw away and distract - on the

AI protocol. You should've seen him. He was bouncing about sniffing flowers. His eyes were this big." She opened her hands wide and held them by her eyes. "It was all, 'Kosta! Don't touch that, it will eat you. No, don't touch that either. Don't pet that giant monster... Like trying to walk a kitten on a leash."

Venturo laughed and then the laugh died. "Why didn't you tell me?"

"I almost did, up in the roof garden. And then you went on about how I had a nice quiet mind."

He groaned. "I was trying to pay you a compliment."

She mimicked him. "'You have such a quiet mind, Claire. I deal all day with people whose brains are noisy.' Was I supposed to come back with, by the way, I can kill you with my brain and I indulge in dirty fantasies about you in my spare time?"

He grabbed her and pinned her down. "I like your dirty fantasies."

She laughed.

"And I like when you laugh." He kissed her. "Mmm."

She untangled herself from him and rolled off the bed. "Come on. I'll show you the split."

"Oh, I'd love to see that." His grin was carnal.

"No, you fool, the cloning technique. Come on."

He got off the bed.

"Bionet hub," she ordered. A section of the wall split, and a small liquid interface terminal emerged, the lid sealed.

"Still sealed," Ven said.

"I was too afraid to log in. Besides, the shell takes a week to rebuild. I didn't want to chance it." She took out two cognizance units from the shelf and tore the plastic.

Ven twisted the lid, breaking the seal. "Some people open wine. We open the hub."

She fitted the unit on him and waited as he fit one on her. It felt oddly symbolic.

The dark tunnel swallowed her, and a moment later she landed next to him into the soft grass. They sat in a jungle clearing, wild bright flowers blooming all around them.

The enormous beast that was Ven stretched, raking the ground with his massive claws. Claire rolled, batting her red paws at the sun rays puncturing the jungle canopy in narrow spears of light.

A deep underground roar made her jump up.

The jungle fell apart, melting. The ground underneath them surged up, the wind pressing on them like a massive hand. Suddenly the movement stopped.

Behind them the ground dropped off in a sheer cliff. They stood on the edge of a wide grassy plateau. A low sound of a gong rang through the world. In the distance a bright star winked, then another, and another. Psychers logging in.

"Cute," Venturo said.

The realization washed over her. "DDS. Pelori came to see me two days ago, trying to buy me. He had sensed the shell on my mind. They must've put a code trap on my access line."

Across the plateau, dust rose. Something massive was moving toward them at top speed.

"Figured," Ven said. "Attacking Guardian was too risky. Castilla must've decided that sooner or later you would log in and alone you'd be the perfect target."

"We can grow wings and glide down off the cliff," Claire said.

He shook his enormous head. "No. I am going to finish this once and for all. But if you want to go -"

"Are you joking? You couldn't drag me away."

The cloud of dust parted and she saw them: an enormous elephantine monster, followed by a huge canine and a flightless bird with fiery plumage. Lim, Pelori, and Castilla.

Claire grinned, displaying her fangs. Fire sheathed Ven.

The monsters were almost upon them.

"Hey," Ven said to her. "Watch this."

Epilogue

From: Lienne Escana
To: Malvina Escana

MALVI, I know you won't believe it, but your son finally found someone. Smart girl, Grade A psycher, perfect manners, you'll love her. Apparently Castilla had the stupidity to attack the two of them in the bionet, and they ended up rampaging through DDS. It was brutal. DDS is still recovering and their stock has fallen 32%. I'd give you the details, but they refuse to talk about it during the work day and at night they hole up in his apartment, drink pink wine, and have sex like two rabid monkeys.

Anyway, if you want Venturo to marry, now is your chance. I've got a scheduling conference set up on Monday, and if we ambush them there with combined forces, I'm sure we can get them to commit to a date. I suggest you make your husband warm up the aerial as soon as you get this.

YOUR LOVING SISTER,
Lienne

A MERE FORMALITY

Chapter 1

The alarm chimed, sending tiny shivers through Deirdre's fingers, coated in liquid interface. Five minutes to the opening speech. "All right, all right." She shrugged the lead-grey metal off her hand and caught her reflection in the mirror. The hair. She had forgotten about her hair.

Her gown looked fantastic. She loved this dress; the cut and color suited her: a shimmering grey-black that caught her breasts, wound about her waist and fell down in clean lines to brush the floor. Unfortunately, the gown alone wouldn't do it. Her hair sat atop her head in an ugly pile, and it was too late to do anything about it. It's your fault, Robert, she thought, pulling out the pins one by one. She dragged the brush through her hair and inspected the result.

Hideous.

That's fine, she decided. Nobody can be expected to be ran ragged for nine straight hours and then attend a banquet looking perfect.

A knock jarred her from her thoughts. "Open!"

The door slid open, revealing Fatima Lee in her navy blue power-dress. Robert's aide-de-camp looked perfect, her hair a glossy black wave, her face fresh as if she had taken a long refreshing nap instead of the grueling administrative marathon.

"Three minutes to opening speech. If we're late, Robert will suffer a deep space fit."

They headed out the door and down the winding hallway at the speed of a brisk march. Unbound by gravity, the makers of the Orbital Embassy had constructed an impossibly tall banquet hall, and the hallway circling it matched it in height. Today the huge walls and ceiling lost in darkness brought a sense of foreboding. Like going through some ancient Temple to be sacrificed.

Fatima's communicator buzzed with the voice of Michel Rashvili. "Where are you? Robert's losing it."

"We'll be there in thirty seconds, tell his Excellency to keep his panties on." Fatima snorted. "I don't get it. The man can negotiate with terrorists with a needle rifle pressed to his temple, but banquets drive him up the wall." "That's because he can't control a banquet," Deirdre murmured. "And the stakes are high." 30 million lives hanging in the balance would give anyone a pause.

They rounded the curve. The huge doors of the banquet chamber waited wide open just ahead, under the banner depicting the Duke of Rodkil, Robert's mentor and veritable legend in the annals of the Diplomatic Corps. Fatima zeroed in on the doors.

Several men dressed in black entered the hallway from a side passage, also aiming for the door. Deirdre caught Fatima's arm. "The Reigh."

The aide-de-camp halted. The Reigh moved in silence, like black ghosts, each carrying a vered, a short ceremonial branch, in their left hand signifying their peaceful intentions. Tradition dictated they stayed silent when in sight of the enemy until given permission to speak by the Lord. For them, everyone is an enemy, Deirdre thought.

They had to be desperate for the money to even enter the Orbital. Unfortunately, taking money for their military services was the very thing that the Reigh doctrine categorically forbade.

A tousled man shot out of the doors at a near run…Michel

Rashvili mumbling into his communicator. As if in slow motion Deirdre saw him crash into the nearest Reigh. The black-gloved hand let go and the sign of peace clattered to the floor. Oh great Lao Tzu.

Michel stumbled, caught himself. His face went slack with shock. A short-range plasma firearm leaped into Fatima's hand almost on its own.

"Michel, kneel!" Deirdre approached and dropped to her knees.

Michel hit the floor next to her. Wide-eyed, he looked at the vered. "I'm so sorry. Should I?" His voice shook.

"No. Keep your head down, don't look them in the eye." Very slowly Deirdre reached and picked up the branch off the floor. Holding it on her open palms, she raised it above her head, like an offering. Their eyes fixed on the floor, they waited. Moments dripped by, long and viscous. Finally the Reigh closest to her stepped forward. Leather brushed her palm, and the Reigh moved on, still silent, into the banquet hall. Deirdre remembered to breathe.

"Sweet Jesus." Michel straightened. "I can't believe I knocked that out of his hand."

"You didn't." Fatima's firearm had vanished. There was no way it could be hidden in that tiny dress. "He dropped it."

"You're kidding me."

"He dropped it," Deirdre confirmed, looking after the Reigh making their way through the banquet hall. "When was the last time you fought in hand to hand combat, Michel?"

The adjutant ran a shaking hand through his hair. "I don't remember."

"They do it every day. Trust me, if that man didn't want to run into you, you wouldn't have touched him in a million years. Go hide somewhere."

"What?"

"Go hide, dimwit." Fatima snorted. "When Robert finds out, he'll blow his core. You want to give him a few hours to cool off."

The words finally made an impact and the adjutant took off down the hallway.

Chapter 2

Deirdre frowned. "We have been tested, and I'm not sure we've passed. Why do I have a feeling this isn't going to end well?"

"Because it won't." Fatima's face was grim. "Let's go." For better or worse they entered the banquet hall.

THE RED-FURRED Vunta officer at Deirdre's left smiled at her, exposing fifty two sharp teeth, arranged in twin rows in his cavernous mouth. The effect was enough to give a hardened Navy veteran a lifetime of nightmares.

"You wook wowery," he offered, sounding very much like a Terran Scottsman with a mouthful of tissue stuffed into his cheeks. He hit her with a direct, unblinking stare.

Trying to dominate. He should know better. "Thank you." She showed him her teeth and glared back.

For a moment they stared eye-to-eye, neither willing to back down. Deirdre ground her teeth. The sound died in the hum of the banquet hall but not before the Vunta heard it. A noise reserved for the alpha of the Vunta society, the grinding had the same effect on the Vunta as the scraping of nails on a glass had on the human ear. The officer wrinkled his muzzle and looked away.

Deirdre glanced across the hall at the Vunta, seated here and there at the tables. Too many flickering ears, too many flashes of teeth, too much animation in the gestures of furry paw-hands. Like sharks smelling blood in the water. What is going on? What do they know that we don't?

She looked to Robert, seated at the head table between the Vunta Ambassador and the elderly lemon-skinned Monrovian with mournful iconic eyes. Sir Robert Sergei Sarvini, Ambassador of the Second Intergalactic Empire to the Branches of Reigh, looked perfect: hair slicked back into a horse tail, handsome face shaven, trim figure sharp in Diplomatic Corps formal midnight blue. Urbane, debonair, eloquent, every inch worthy of the long list of titles attached to his name.

Robert's food lay untouched on his plate. Officially the banquet was thrown in honor of the successful treaty negotiations between the Monrovians and the Vunta Caliphate, for which the Empire, in the form of Robert, had provided a neutral meeting ground. Unofficially, Robert wanted to woo the Reigh. Unfortunately, he was stuck at the head table, sandwiched between the two treaty partners.

Their stares connected and in his eyes she read a confirmation. Yes, something's up. No, we don't know what. We can do nothing about it. Just sit tight and wait.

Deirdre sighed. There were four parties to this dance: the Vunta Caliphate, the Monrovian Republic, the Empire, and the Reigh. Each wanted something and would claw all others bloody to get it. All she wanted to do was to prevent a massacre.

She looked to the guest of honor table where Lord Nagrad of the Reigh sat with Nina on one side and a white-furred Vunta dignitary on the other. The rest of the Reigh formed a line behind the table. None but the Lord had chosen to sit down. None ate or drank. A line from the Reigh Codex popped into her head: I will consume no food in the house of my enemy…

Nagrad's scarred face was grim. Had he been from an inner Imperial world, she would've guessed him at eighty or ninety. Her painstaking research put him at closer to sixty. The only Reigh lord in the history of his people to entertain the idea of cooperation. His wife was dead. His entire family consisted of his son. And the Vunta Raiders were very afraid of him.

The Vunta dignitary shot Nagrad a toothy smile and said something. Nina cut in, smooth, breathtaking like a golden angel against the backdrop of black. Deirdre felt a stab of jealousy right in the stomach. Nina's perfect six foot and one inch tall figure was wrapped in a strapless gown of champagne-colored lace, accented with complex swirls of golden thread. The dress hugged her like a glove. The color perfectly complemented her light blonde hair and light bronze complexion.

"Why couldn't we have her job?" Fatima murmured at her right.

"Because we don't score 8:13 on the proportion scale," Deirdre said. "And because we haven't been trained as escorts and we don't have a perfect recall."

"Bullshit," Fatima said. "You know you could do what she does with your eyes closed. You're a freaking cultural attaché. You know more about the Reigh than all of us combined. You should be picking the Reigh Lord's brains, not she."

"She knows what she's doing. My job is to compile and analyze the information. Her job is to keep the object of her attention enraptured." And it would be an incredibly difficult task, considering the strictness of the Reigh rules of conduct. Nothing off-color. Not a hint, not a joke, not even an idea of impropriety. No reference to sex, religion, or politics. Deirdre smiled. "I'm perfectly happy to advise her from the sidelines."

Fatima sneered. "You have no ambition. In the next life, you'll be reborn as a tea kettle."

Nina reached for a small appetizer and artfully offered it to the Reigh Lord. He accepted the tiny twisted dough puff and bit into it. Nina continued talking. She had a way to totally engage a person in conversation, until speaking to her appeared to be a reward in itself.

The Reigh Lord finished the puff. A nervous tick jerked his face once, twice. A grimace twisted his features, baring his teeth. He arched his back, biting at the empty air. His hands flailed, knocking over the goblets and plates. A spasm gripped his body. He shuddered, froze, and fell back against his seat, foam sliding from his lips down his chin.

For a moment absolute silence claimed the hall. And then chaos broke.

THE SITUATION MADE ABSOLUTELY no sense.

Deirdre dipped her fingers into the interface. The liquid metal coated her hand, climbing from her fingertips all the way to her wrist. It slid between her fingers, slightly cold, dry but slippery with silky smoothness, the way very fine sand might feel if individual sand granules were perfectly round. As the synaptic implants under her skin made connections with free floating nanoclusters, she felt her hand—skin, muscle, ligament, and bone —stretch impossibly far. She thought of the archive. The four petals of the unit ignited with pale green, and the huge collection of files, the sum total of her research and archival documents, flared into existence, projected into space above the petals.

Ten feet away Robert slumped in the chair. In the corner Nina rubbed her face with her hands. The room was dim, the huge communication screens on the wall silent and dark, all except the one on the right side, showing the map of the sector. In the center of the map hung the Colchida Cluster, three stars, eleven habitable worlds total, four warp points, thirty million colonists. It used to belong to the Monrovian Republic. Situated too far from Monrovian industrial centers, it was all but worthless to the Republic. But to the Empire, the Cluster was a diamond in rough. Had the Empire been given a chance to develop the Cluster, it would've become the biggest industrial and commercial base of the sector.

Unfortunately the Vunta Caliphate very much enjoyed raiding the Cluster while it was in the Monrovian possession. The numerous stars of the Caliphate, tinted with pale blue to show the territory boundaries, hung in the corner of the map like a storm cloud. It would take the Empire at least two decades to build up the defenses of the Cluster to a survivable level. Until then, the only guard against the Vunta were the Reigh, a thin ribbon of worlds tinted with green.

The Vunta wanted to make a last run at the Cluster, stripping it of all valuables. Hundreds of lives would be lost. The Empire would threaten war and the Caliphate would back off with apologies, but the budding economy of the Cluster would be wrecked. It would take decades and billions to recover.

The Empire needed to protect the Cluster. The Reigh needed the money. But the Reigh doctrine forbade trading payment for military service. And so the staff of the Embassy had to figure out how to skirt the Reigh doctrine. To find an underhanded way to exchange money for protection with the people, who were forbidden to become mercenaries. Now it would never happen.

They were responsible for the safety of 30 million colonists and they blew it. The thought made her stomach lurch.

Deirdre sank deeper into the interface, both arms up to the elbow, speed-reading through the flurry of documents and her notes. She couldn't quite put her finger on it, but she was sure if she just figured out what it was her subconscious was trying to tell her, the situation would become logical.

Fatima moved on quiet feet to stand at Robert's side. "Would you like some tea?"

"What I would like is to travel back in time twenty-four hours and strangle the sushi chef. How could we not know Nagrad was allergic to redfish caviar?"

Deirdre heard the question. It sank in slowly, fighting its way through her focus.

"Numerous reasons," she said, still reading. "Nagrad could have not known he was allergic. He could have deliberately hidden the allergy so it wouldn't be used against him. He could've been distracted by Nina and not realized what he was eating. The Vunta could've poisoned him. Your theory is as good as mine—all of them are total rubbish."

Robert startled. "Why?"

The tone of his voice snapped her out of her search. "Because the Reigh are suspicious paranoiacs, who also happen to be very poor actors."

She tossed the recording of the banquet to one of the side screens, fast-forwarding to the right frame. "Look at him. Yes, he's taking pains to listen to Nina, but he's hardly absorbed. He can't even pretend to be interested enough to fool a casual observer. He's definitely not distracted enough to ignore poisonous food. Look at the line of faces behind him. They are about as relaxed as stone idols on New Barbar and they are watching him so hard, they don't even blink. Do you really think they would let him put something bad in his mouth? Not really. Nor would they let the Vunta mysteriously sprinkle something on his food. This whole thing makes no sense at all."

The main screen ignited and the face of Timur Gonzales came into the view. The Chief of Security looked slightly baffled, hooded dark eyes melancholy, long phlegmatic face relaxed, as if he just woke up from a long nap in sunshine. It made total sense that the Reigh would demand communication through him…the Branch Nagrad and the Empire were now technically in the state of war. Unfortunately he had about as much diplomatic ability as Deirdre herself.

Timur dragged his fingers across his chin, stroking an imaginary beard. "We have contact."

Robert looked up. "Patch them through."

"They won't talk to you," Deirdre said, almost at the same time as Timur.

"Why not?"

"Because you're technically responsible for Nagrad's death. They would be honor-bound to kill you on sight," Deirdre said.

"What she said," Timur added.

Robert growled. "Fine, patch them through on the side screen as a closed feed."

"They've already delivered the terms."

The veins in Robert's temples bulged. "For Zeus's sake, would you stop wasting my time then and give me the bloody recording?"

A harsh-faced Reigh filled the screen. "You've robbed our Branch of a great man. You must atone. The blood-tree must be replenished. You will provide a woman for Lord Nagrad so an heir can be born. And you will pay a dowry. A very large dowry, for the insult was grave. Thirty billion units."

Deirdre blinked. Brilliant. Lao Tzu, that was simply brilliant.

Robert exhaled. "Out of the question! The entire Nagrad Branch can survive for a decade on that money. Tell him…"

Deirdre cut in. "Robert, a marriage would make you related. He would be honor-bound to protect your possessions."

She watched the thought sink in. Robert's face took on an intense look of a hound closing in for a kill. "Ask him if the marriage would mean Branch Nagrad would protect the Cluster in the event of a raid or invasion."

Timur intoned the words. Deirdre tuned him out, going back to her notes. She already knew the answer.

"Yes," Timur relayed.

Robert leaned back. "So here it is. Nagrad Junior doesn't waste time, does he? Thirty billion is a bit steep, but it's doable."

"I'll do it. It's my responsibility." Nina rose with dignity, her voice hoarse. "You may tell Lord Nagrad that I accept his proposal."

"He doesn't want you," Timur said. "Well, who does he want?" Robert asked.

Chapter 3

Deirdre finally hit on the correct recording, thirty-two years ago, one of the first contact missions to the Reigh. The ceremonial trading of the swords, and sharing of the food. She zoomed the picture, focusing on the platter before the Survey Captain and a young-looking Reigh warrior…

Robert's face penetrated the projection. She looked up at him.

"Deirdre," he said, his voice quiet and earnest. "Do you remember your oath to the Diplomatic Corps? The part where you promised to dedicate your body and mind…" "To serve to the most of my ability and to sacrifice my life should my duty demand it. Of course I remember." Robert tried to pick up her hands but they were covered in the liquid interface. He settled on holding her shoulders instead. "How do you feel about sacrifice in a form of a marriage?"

"Lord Nagrad desires a meeting with his bride," the Reigh said. "He wants to determine that she is of sound body and free of mental retardation. She must be ready in one hour."

Robert wheeled about. "Our shuttle. Tell him our people are coming with her and we want her safely delivered back or the deal is off."

After a momentary pause, the Reigh inclined his dark head. "Agreed."

THE HALLWAYS of the Nagrad keep looked unlike anything Deirdre had imagined. She had pictured bleak dark walls; instead she found wall-long windows and a palette ranging from rust to fresh mint green. As she walked down the corridor between Timur and Johanna Bray, the red rays of the rising sun danced on the wall and slid on her gray dress, adding color to the fabric.

It didn't make her feel any better.

She recalled Robert's briefing: You're going there to haggle. Get him down to twenty billion. Take the initiative and don't let him control the conversation. I'm sorry I can't be there with you, but I promise you, I won't send you to him without backup again. This is just the first step, Deirdre. We have a long way to go before we'll agree on the amount.

The fact that she was being appraised like a cow at market apparently didn't bother him at all.

Their escort, a Reigh woman in black leather, led them to a wooden door and stepped inside, closing it behind her.

"Why me?" Deirdre murmured.

"Because you're hot," Timur said. "Because he hates blondes. Because a bug bit him this morning when he got out of bed."

"He had it on the first one," Johanna said. "You're pretty hot. Don't worry, we'll get you back up to the Orbital in one piece."

The door opened and their escort invited them into the room with a sweep of her hand.

Deirdre stepped through. Despite the large window, gloom pooled in the corners and snuck across soft rugs. A single table stood in the middle of the room, lit by the soft yellow light of a cluster lamp. Two chairs flanked the table. In a far chair sat a Reigh. Lean. Dressed in black like all of them. Black hair, cut short.

He sat just outside the circle of light, and shadows masked his face. What a cheap trick.

The escort moved forward, silent like a shadow, and held the second chair out for her. Here we go. Her knees trembled. This is so stupid. Why am I scared?

She forced herself to walk across the carpet. Timur followed. The Reigh gave him a flat stare and the chief of security halted a few feet away. Deirdre sat.

"Lord Nagrad, I presume." Her voice sounded almost normal.

The Reigh inclined his head. She could see him now. He had a hard face, not handsome but not unpleasant. Square jaw, strong nose. The same sharp intelligence she saw in his father's eyes showed full force in his. How old is he? Thirty?

"I am..."

"Deirdre Lebed. I know."

The sound of his voice almost made her jump. She looked past him, trying to collect herself, and saw four shadows in the depth of the room. Bodyguards.

Take away the initiative. Right. "Would you mind if I asked you a question?"

"Please, feel free."

"Why choose a foreign wife? One who is unfamiliar with the traditions and culture? Why not just take the monetary restitution?"

He braided the fingers of his hands into a single fist. "To accept a bribe for the loss of life is forbidden by the doctrine. Besides, a woman from outside the Reigh has several advantages. The man is the trunk of a family, but the woman is its root. In our society, men own the children and the means of war. Everything else is owned by the woman. And too often a woman's first loyalty is to her mother instead of her husband. It tends to make matters...complicated. A woman of the foreign blood has no one to turn to. She would exist solely at the mercy of her husband."

Fantastic. This conversation was going a long way to allay her concerns about becoming a bride.

"And," the Reigh Lord permitted himself a small smile. "Our traditions are rather binding. There are certain things a man could ask of foreign woman that would be considered unclean by the women of the Reigh."

"What kind of things?"

"Things of sexual nature. Do you consider yourself open-minded in those matters, Lady Deirdre? Would you do all those things at my request?"

If he was willing to walk down the road, it was perfectly fine with her. With Reigh being as rigid as they were, it was likely he'd bail first. Deirdre arched her eyebrows. "Very few women within the Empire do all things, Lord Nagrad. I cannot confirm what I may or may not do without knowing what you have in mind. Would you be more specific?"

She smiled and waited for him to back off. "Would you suck my cock?" he asked.

She stared at him for a long moment, trying to make sure she didn't mishear. Behind her someone made a strangled noise.

The Reigh Lord waited for her answer. His face was perfectly solemn.

"Well." She cleared her throat, desperately hoping she didn't blush. "I suppose that could be...hrhm arranged under certain circumstances. Is there any...other requests you would like to make?"

He raised his hand. One of the shadows detached itself from the gloom and brought a platter with a thin pseudo-paper magazine. She hadn't seen pseudo-paper since her days at Altair museums during her graduate on the Colonial Journalism.

Nagrad took the magazine off the platter and put it on the table. The digital photograph on the cover left no doubt as to what kind of a publication it was. He flipped the pages and pushed the magazine toward her. "Would you do this?"

"Yes."

He flipped another page. "This one?"

"Possibly."

"This one?"

She felt the blush creeping onto her cheeks. "Yes."

"What about this one?"

She squinted, trying to make sense of the naked shapes. "Is that even possible? Wouldn't you have to have low G for this?"

"Or a very strong woman."

"I'm not sure I'm that strong."

"I suppose we could arrange a shuttle trip then," he offered.

"No, thank you. Thirty billion is an outrageously large sum."

"You think so? Considering the scale of the injury, I believe it's just right." He flipped the page. "How about this one?"

ROBERT'S FACE WAS INCREDULOUS. "You didn't drop him at all? Not even by half a bil? Oh Hermes, a child could've done better."

Deirdre threw the recorder onto the table. Nagrad's face, frozen on the screen, mocked her with grey eyes. "What do you want from me, Robert? Every time I tried to bring up the money, he would show me more porn. The man asked me if I would suck his cock! How do you counter that?"

A soft voice interrupted, "By saying, 'That would depend on the size of your instrument, my lord. Would you care to take off your pants so I can determine if it would be a good fit?'"

Robert bent in a half, "My lord."

She turned to see an older man in a soft green tunic. He gave her a light smile, as if he was too polite to laugh at his own off-color joke.

"Holy crap, the Duke of Rodkil." Fatima's heels clicked together.

Deirdre bowed. The living legend placed his hand onto her shoulder. Imposing on the portraits, in person he appeared rather slight, short with a narrow, bird-boned frame. "No need to bend your back, my dear. I understand Robert called me as soon as he knew, but despite all of our progress, there are times when the interstellar travel isn't quite fast enough." He nodded at Nagrad on the screen. "A very shrewd man. Let's see if we can cut him down a bit, shall we? I'll need all of the background you have."

DEIRDRE SHRUGGED the interface off her hands and leaned back against the seat. Her head throbbed. The ancient diplomat was still speed-reading, submerged in the interface up to his elbow.

"What's the significance of kneeling? Submission?"

She rubbed her temples. "Not exactly, Your Grace."

"Jason," he corrected.

"Jason," she repeated, trying to ignore the absurdity of referring to a recipient of the Diamond Sword by his first name. "The Reigh don't submit. Not even in battle—when they surrender, they raise their hands to the sides, daring a thrust to the stomach. The kneeling… It's more a gesture of ultimate respect. A Reigh kneels only before his Lord and only once, at the acceptance into service. A Reigh Lord kneels before no one."

"A quaint culture. So many references to the vegetative symbolism."

"Yes."

The Duke…Jason glanced at her. "You should sleep, my dear. You look exhausted. He's likely to call for another meeting tomorrow."

She sighed. "Why? I couldn't haggle him down. He'd be smart to avoid us so he can hold on to the original sum."

"But he knows you don't control the proverbial purse strings. He's perfectly aware the real fight is ahead and he doesn't want to give us enough time to regroup."

She sighed. "He caught me off-guard. I expected coldness, some sort of brutal physical test, perhaps a ritual where I'd have to untangle tree branches without breaking the leaves or untie an impossible knot. I didn't expect dirty pictures. It goes against everything I know about them. It makes me question my assumptions."

Jason shook his head. "What I've seen so far is both thorough and well documented. Your conclusions are logical and, I wager, quite accurate. Robert is very lucky to have you, and he knows it, otherwise he wouldn't have called me." The Duke chuckled. "Quite a hit to his pride, to have to call your former mentor out of retirement. But back to the Reigh, don't doubt the entire body of your research on the basis of Lord Nagrad. In diplomacy, like in great many other things, the rules of engagement survive only until one remarkable person decides to break them. It's just our luck we stumbled across such a person."

"That, and the fact that I'm a lousy diplomat."

"To each his own. You're an excellent analyst. Not everyone is born with the gift of snappy comeback. But you should rest. And don't worry, we may yet get you out of this mess."

THIS TIME the meeting fell onto afternoon, and the sunlight filled the room. Nagrad waited in precisely the same position Deirdre had seen him the first time. "Greetings, Lady Deirdre. And Your Grace."

Jason smiled. "I wasn't aware I'm well know to the Reigh."

"You are," Nagrad assured him.

"Very well, Lord Nagrad." Jason rubbed his hands together. "In that case shall we dispense with preliminary niceties? Let's talk money."

"Indeed."

They launched into the foray like two warriors, amidst clashing blades and thudding shields. By the second hour Deirdre lost the thread of the argument. By the fourth she caught herself dosing off.

Nagrad's voice snapped her from her reverie. "I do believe the lady is tired. Let us take a break." He offered her his hand. "Would my lady care for some fresh air?"

To say no would've been an insult. She put her hand in his and let him lead her out to the balcony. Big enough for a decent size party, the semicircular balcony extended out good twenty five meters. Nagrad maneuvered all the way to its farthest point and stopped at an ornate amber and white rail. The keep protruded from the side of the mountain and as she looked down below to where the forest shimmered awash with green leaves, a curious feeling of peace filled Deirdre. Bright blue and red birds flittered from branch to branch. Somewhere a distant relative of the Vunta howled once. She inhaled the air. It tasted sweet.

"Beautiful," she murmured. "I forgot how lovely the planetside can be."

"It's home," he said simply, putting the world into a single word. Deirdre leaned on the rail. "Why me?"

"Because you're attractive," he said. "And I greatly admire your body." She blushed.

"Of work," he added and offered her his reader. A list of recent publications lit the screen. The top one…

"This hasn't been publicized. It's classified information." She took the reader and tapped the top title with the stylus. Here it was, the entire contents of her Reigh research. "How did you get this?"

"It was brought to my attention by a party concerned that we may have a loose mouth in our midst."

"You tapped the Embassy's network." She stared at him stunned. Lao-Tzu, what else he could have access to?

"It wasn't that difficult actually." He shrugged. "I can't afford informants in my branch, no more than you can tolerate the blame for my father's death."

"I had no informants." She handed the reader back to him.

"I realized that once I'd read through your analysis. To have deduced that much from external indicators is remarkable."

The extent of his arrogance was even more remarkable. Deirdre looked at him. "Then perhaps you would enjoy another deduction." She slid the square of a reader card from her data bracelet and snapped it into the reader. The recording of a peace meeting from three decades ago filled the screen. "This is the Survey Captain Sean Kozlov. And this, I believe, is your father. They are performing a peace ritual—they have fished together and now they are sharing their catch." She tapped the screen, forcing it to zoom. "They are eating redfish. And redfish caviar."

Nagrad watched the screen. The impassive mask slipped and in his face she saw profound sadness.

"Your father wasn't allergic to caviar," she said.

"My father was born without immunity to black moss." Nagrad kept his gaze on the reader. "A genetic failure, a mutation that for some reason wasn't detected. He had survived for sixty four years without contracting the infection. We didn't realize he was sick until he began coughing black dust. Very rare in these times, unfortunately, it still happens."

The black moss was incurable. Two month incubation period and then a soft death, as the victim fell asleep to never awaken. Instead of passing on in his bed, the Reigh Lord died in agony amidst strangers. "He took his own life."

Nagrad leaned back. "He felt his death must serve the Branch. The only difficulty lay in finding the poison that would imitate an allergic reaction to redfish. The death didn't happen as quickly as we had hoped."

The realization struck her. "You were there," she said. "Were you the one who took the vered off my hand?"

He closed his eyes for the briefest of moments. "Yes."

"You stood there and you watched your father die."

"He was my Lord. I honored his wishes."

"He died to give you an excuse to take a bribe from the Empire."

Nagrad's face gained a dangerous edge. "Yes. And the Branch desperately needs the money. And you may be assured, my Lady, that I will do everything in my power to squeeze every last unit I can from your realm. To do any less would be to dishonor his death."

He took the card from the reader and offered it to her, but she closed his fist about it. "It belongs to you."

Before he could say anything else, she shook her head. "I understand, Lord Nagrad. I truly do."

"I suppose you despise me."

"No. I admire you." She walked away so he wouldn't see her face.

THE EVENING BROUGHT a cup of fragrant tea and a knock on Deirdre's door. "Come in," she yelled, wishing with all her being the visitor would go away. Nina Carrest entered the room. Dressed in a soft robe that looked like it had been slept in, her hair pulled back from her face in a hastily made pony tail, Nina looked radiantly beautiful.

It was simply not fair that a woman should do absolutely nothing and look this good. "I'm not sure why I'm here." Nina shifted uncomfortably.

"Please come in."

They sat on the soft circular couch and drank tea together. "I feel responsible." Nina rubbed her left temple. "I don't want you to think that I came here because I feel guilty and I want you to tell me it will be fine and it's not my fault. I just...it should've been me."

"It would've been me anyway." Deirdre sat her teacup back onto the table. "The Reigh had hacked the Orbital's database. I'm apparently the only one who didn't know this. Robert fed them my research on purpose. Lord Nagrad very much wanted to meet me. He would've found an occasion to do so, one way or the other."

"Still, I fed his father that appetizer..."

Deirdre offered her a smile. "I wouldn't worry about that. The old Lord Nagrad didn't die from an allergic attack. He was terminally ill and had taken poison so his son would have pretext to ask the Empire for the monetary compensation. His son was right there among the guards. He watched him die."

Nina paled. "That's monstrously cold blooded."

Deirdre sighed. Some things were harder to explain than others. She pulled her portable to her. A small part of her rebelled against interfacing this late. She had wanted the evening to last, to drink her tea, and enjoy the few minutes of comfort, to work on herself by being still. But the need to explain nagged her into dipping her hand into the liquid metal. She watched it creep up to mid-palm…no need for more…and waited until the sensation of stretching subsided enough to speak.

"The first colonists to have settled on some of the Reigh worlds pre-Second Empire were the Sureks. The word 'lahiko', the Reigh's substitution for "clan", is thought to have been a corruption of Surek Luh-iko, meaning literally 'branch.' However, if you ask a Reigh to pronounce it, he will say, 'Lehgio.' An almost perfectly preserved, true Latin pronunciation of legion."

Deirdre played with the interface and it projected a small map of the Reigh territory. "During the Melasyan conflict, a large part of Melasyus's army broke off, upset by his failure to secure peace. At this point they had been unpaid for over five standard years. They hadn't seen their families. Most of them didn't have families since the Planars had wiped out planet after planet with their toxins. They'd had enough and they took their ships and left. Seven legions."

She highlighted the home worlds of the seven branches of the Reigh one by one. "They were hardened veterans, disciplined, supreme warriors, whom Melasyus strove to make into 'New Romans'. All they wanted was peace."

Nina's gaze was fixed on the map. She refilled their cups without looking.

"They came here?"

"I think so. There are more factors in play here than just a single word. For example, these branches on Nagrad's standard. If we take off the leaves" …she called up a standard and swiped the abundance of stylized leaves from the branches… "and we have the Roman numeral XXIV. The twenty-fourth legion. And so on. My theory is that the legionnaires put as much distance as they could between themselves and Melasyus' ambitions and settled here, mixing with native Surek population. Thirty years ago they were found. Only eight generations since they had left. They are paranoid, extremely martially proficient, and ruled by a doctrine of personal discipline and distrust of outsiders."

"I see."

"The legionnaires had stripped several worlds before they perpetrated their escape. Their descendants stretched those supplies for a long time," Deirdre continued. "But they lacked the expertise to really build an industrial base. I've pulled the logs of their known purchases and ran a projection analysis. They are adept at keeping the fleet and armaments going, but they are rapidly depleting their supplies. Chances are they don't have access to tech developed in the last two hundred years. Also the fact that Lord Nagrad hadn't undergone a genetic screening leads me to believe they're running out of medical equipment. They need vaccines. They need production facilities. They need new tech, but they don't have an overabundance of natural resources nor do they have access to some unique goods. They can't make their money in trade. In fact, the only resource they can export is themselves…they are superior warriors. Unfortunately their doctrine forbids them to do exactly that. They must fight for a cause. If this continues…"

"They will be overrun by the Vunta," Nina said.

Deirdre nodded and shrugged the interface from her hand. "They must find a way to obtain financial resources without breaking the foundation of their society. Or they must give up being who they are. Lord Nagrad came up with a short-term fix. I believe his solution cost his son a great deal of pain."

Nina looked at her. "Tell me about him."

Deirdre thought about it. "Very smart. He has very light eyes, grey with a little bit of green. He's tall. He bends slightly toward you when he speaks. He has large hands and almost never gesticulates. When you speak to him, you get a sense that if he hates you, he'd kill you in a second, but if he likes you, he would do all he could to keep you from harm. It's a curious feeling."

Nina was smiling.

"Did I say something funny?"

"Not at all. Will you really marry him?"

That was a question she had successfully avoided asking herself for two days now. "I don't see how I have any choice in the matter. If I didn't have to marry him, I would've requested an extension anyway. The research material I had compiled here is my best work. I want to know more about them. Looks like I'll get to, just not in a way I had planned."

The comscreen behind her erupted in a series of beeps and almost immediately somebody hammered on her door. She ordered it open, and Robert burst into the room.

"Get dressed! The Vunta overbid us!"

"What?"

"The Vunta just offered Nagrad the thirty billion he wanted in a Brotherhood Pact. He gets exclusive rights to raiding on the fourth world of the Colchida Cluster. We must bid higher, but I have to get approval before I can commit. It will take the com launch at least twenty eight standard hours to reach us with the answer. We must stall until the Treasury approves the expense. We have eight hours until the sun rises to come up with a plan."

Deirdre crossed her arms on her chest. "What do you mean stall?"

"He'll want this matter concluded now, before the Vunta back off, but he can't just back out of the marriage, so he'll demand a higher amount and when we fail to deliver, he will claim to be gravely insulted."

"She could pretend to be sick," Nina said.

"No, then he'll claim we're insulting him by withholding her. It has to be something else, something he can't weasel out of."

An idea snapped together. So simple and so ironic. Deirdre smiled. "Robert?"

"What?"

"How much smut do we have in our databanks?"

"I FEEL DIRTY." Fatima laid her head back. "I don't think I can take anymore."

"Found another one," Michel Rashvili announced. "The man on the back, legs bent, the woman holds his hands on the sides and squats onto his…"

"The amazon," Deirdre and Nina said at the same time.

"Did that one," Robert said.

"I thought the amazon was the one in a chair." Michel yawned.

"No, that's side-saddle." Nina yawned too.

"Has anyone actually done the amazon? I mean like in real life?" Michel wondered.

"I have." Duke of Rodkil yawned. "It's overrated."

Deirdre blinked her eyes, trying to stay awake. Whatever embarrassment she had possessed had fled hours ago.

Robert surveyed the room strewn in pornography sheets and sex toys. "It looks like we had an orgy." He stifled a yawn, gave up and yawned. "Now look what you're started, Rashvili. Don't you know yawning is contagious? We all need a nap."

Nina put her head down and snored.

"Highly appropriate post-orgy, I would say," His Grace murmured.

The comscreen flared and the face of the chief of security came into the view. Nina jerked awake.

"We have contact with the Reigh. They want the bride and they want her now." Timur squinted. "What exactly have you all been doing?"

THE BOOSTER SHOT coursed through Deirdre's veins, spreading a slightly cool sensation all the way from her toes to her scalp. She felt light as a feather. Twelve hours from now she would pay the price by passing out, but for now she felt fantastic.

The elation evaporated when she entered the meeting room. The Reigh guard had been doubled. Nagrad's face promised a storm.

"Are you prepared to accept my terms?"

The question wasn't aimed at her, but the harsh tone lanced her anyway.

"Of course, Lord Nagrad," Jason smoothly said.

"Thirty billion?" The disbelief was plain on Nagrad's face.

"Indeed. However, before the moneys and the lady can exchange hands, there is a small matter that requires your attention. A mere formality."

"What matter?"

The Duke smiled. "In accordance with the formal union contract, the bride requests a full accounting of her duties."

"I've delivered the full accounting during our first meeting."

Not even a single glance in her direction. I am just an animal to be sold and bought. "Yes, but the accounting states, and I quote, '...and to not shun the husband's request in the bedroom, lest she sabotage the begetting of an heir.' This fails to specify the exact nature of your attentions."

"This was also covered in our first meeting."

"But my lord," she said, keeping her voice as sweet as she could. "That was but a very small part. The subject must be explored fully before I commit to you. I have a right to know what is required of me."

"We've taken the liberty of preparing a short list of all 'duties' known to the bride." With the elegance of a dancer, Jason slid the reader card onto the table. "All that remains is for us to examine each entry and to determine whether or not it will enter into accounting. Should you require anything beyond what is detailed here, we will do our best to incorporate it into our list."

Nagrad slid the card into his reader. It took him a good minute to scroll to the end of the list. His eyes blazed. "How many entries are here?"

"Five hundred and forty five." The Duke's voice couldn't have been sweeter.

"I request all of them," Nagrad said.

"In accordance to entry two hundred and three, will you then submit to having a cast of your anal canal so the dildo employed to penetrate your anus can be made to perfect proportions?"

The Reigh bodyguards froze.

Nagrad read the entry. "I won't be requesting that one."

Deirdre leaned forward. "With all due respect, my lord, I insist you review each one to avoid such misunderstandings."

He finally turned to her. "I refuse to submit to this idiocy. The list could take days to review."

"It's my right under the law. You must review the list with the witnesses present. You have made an offer of a formal commitment. It cannot be withdrawn lightly."

She could almost hear him grinding his teeth. "You are not a Reigh. You have no rights."

"Yes, I do. You gave them to me when you delivered the statement of full accounting of my duties and requested a dowry. You have followed the law up to this point as if I was a Reigh bride. Does the doctrine exist only until it suits you, my Lord?"

For a moment she thought he'd reach across the table and strangle her. Instead he sat back. His face relaxed… it must've taken a monumental effort of will on his part… and the Reigh lord picked up the reader. "Very well. The first section is titled 'Terms and Devices'. I believe we can skip that one."

"Would my lord care to define the term anal plug?" Deirdre asked. "How about the difference between the soft and a hard one?"

If his eyes could shoot lightning, she would've been fried on the spot.

"Very well then," His Grace announced with a placating smile.

"Term number one: penis. Also known as dick, cock, Johnson, lance, sword, thruster, little soldier..."

Deirdre leaned toward. "You may want to call for some refreshments, my lord. It will be a very long day."

Four hours later Nagrad tossed his reader onto the table. "I need some fresh air."

He strode onto the balcony. Deirdre rose, stretching, and went outside also.

The second she stepped out of the room, Nagrad took her by the elbow. "Come with me, my Lady."

His touch on her arm was very light, yet she knew with absolute certainty she couldn't get away. He led her to the farthest point of the balcony out of ear shot of the bodyguards within the room. "It's you," he said. "I know it's you. You came up with this farce."

"What gives you that idea?"

"You were gloating in every second of it. Why are you doing this?"

"I simply want to know what's required of me."

He turned away from her, plainly trying to keep control of himself. "This matter could be settled later. It's of no consequence."

"It's of a great consequence to me. You opened the door, all I had to do was walk through it."

"I opened the door?" he snarled.

"Temper, temper, my Lord. I'm sure your guards would rush to my rescue if you were to choke me. Patience is a virtue."

He stared at her. "God preserve the man who makes an enemy of you." He turned on his heel and stalked off.

Deirdre sighed and went back to the room. As she slumped into her chair, His Grace leaned to her. "How did it go?"

"My future husband hates me with a passion of a thousand stars," she said. The Duke gently patted her hand. "We'll get through this."

"That's what I'm afraid of."

"Entry number three hundred and twelve: Multiple partners." The Duke droned on.

Deirdre put her head onto her hands. Post-booster cooldown required at least twelve hours of sleep. She barely got eight before the Reigh demanded her presence. Her head hurt. Her ears were filled with something soft and mushy. Across the table Nagrad looked exhausted. The two Reigh witnesses, picked by him from the bodyguard, didn't look much better.

"Subsection A. Two male partners and one female partner."

"Pass," Nagrad called. There were deep bags under his eyes.

"Let it be known that Lord Nagrad abandons all claim to the act described in entry number three hundred and twelve, subsection A and all the subsequent positions described or listed under subsection A."

"So noted," the witnesses intoned.

Everyone made the appropriate notations in their copy of the list.

"Subsection B: Two female partners and one male partner." The Duke waited for a moment, but Nagrad appeared absorbed in his reader.

"Position one: the male partner assumes horizontal position with his back to the surface. The first female partner kneels…"

Deirdre rolled her eyes. Just pass now, you know you can't take it in front of the witnesses. Nagrad listened to the description with the look of somber concentration. "Pass," he said finally.

"Let it be known that Lord Nagrad abandons all claim to the act described in entry number three hundred and twelve, subsection B, position one."

Deirdre stuck her tongue out at him.

Nagrad mouthed, "After we're married."

"So noted," the witnesses mumbled.

"Position number two: the first female partner clasps the male partner's…"

The Duke's comlink beeped. "Excuse me. It appears I have an urgent call." He strode away onto the balcony.

Deirdre put her head onto the table with a soft bump. Marry me off, I don't care. I just want some sleep.

She heard the Duke's footsteps. They stopped next to her. "Thirty five billion," he said softly.

She raised her head. Nagrad sat very still.

"That's an extraordinary offer." A slow kind smile softened the Duke's face. "You won't get a better one."

"Done," Nagrad breathed.

There. The odd look on his face, relief mixed with surprise, brought out her own smile. We did it, she thought. We saved the cluster and we saved you and your people. She watched the beginning of a smile curl his lips. In this moment of joy, he seemed almost vulnerable.

"Thirty six billion, if you abandon your claim to Deirdre," the Duke said. Cold washed over her. That's it. It's over. I will never see him again. "No," Nagrad said.

"We both know it was never about the girl. Let her go."

Nagrad's face snapped back into an impenetrable mask. "She stays or the deal is off."

The Duke drew himself to his full height, suddenly regal and terrifying. "Ask yourself, would you truly force yourself on this woman?"

Nagrad looked at her. "Do you want out?"

"She has a brilliant career ahead of her," the Duke said. "Don't stand in her way." Nagrad took her hand and swept her off the chair. "A minute of your time, my Lady." He pushed past the Duke and drew her outside.

I'm so sick of running onto this balcony, a thought flashed through her head.

Nagrad ran his hand through his hair. "I'm past my undergrowth years."

"I'm sorry?"

"I'm not an adolescent anymore. What I mean to say is, women no longer unsettle me."

He held up his hands, seemingly lost or words. "This is harder than I thought."

He looked so lost that she laughed softly. "Did I unsettle you?"

"Yes," he said, relieved. "I...miss you when you're away. I think of you. I don't want you to leave."

"You were ready to trade me in for the Vunta billions."

"Yes," he admitted. "I would've done whatever was best for the Branch. What would you have done in my place?"

Deirdre looked at the forest beyond the balcony. "In your place I would've auctioned myself off if I thought I'd get more than one bid."

The Duke and the bodyguards were watching them. "I wish I knew what to say," Nagrad said. "But if you give me a chance, I think I would come to love you very much. Marry me and I promise you I'll be as loyal to you as my father was to me. I'll do everything I can to make you happy."

The way he looked at her made Deirdre's heart flutter.

He took a deep breath and glanced at the audience waiting in the room. "They will only see it once."

Slowly, deliberately he knelt before her. "Stay," he said. "Please."

"Well that won't do," she murmured. "The Reigh Lord doesn't kneel before anyone." She knelt next to him. "That's better."

"Is that a yes?"

She brushed his lips with hers and he kissed her, her mouth eager and warm. "It's a yes," she murmured when they came up for air. "On one condition. You have to tell me your name, because I am not moaning 'Lord Nagrad' on our wedding night."

Also by Ilona Andrews

Kate Daniels World

BLOOD HEIR

Kate Daniels Series

MAGIC BITES

MAGIC BLEEDS

MAGIC BURNS

MAGIC STRIKES

MAGIC MOURNS

MAGIC BLEEDS

MAGIC DREAMS

MAGIC SLAYS

GUNMETAL MAGIC

MAGIC GIFTS

MAGIC RISES

MAGIC BREAKS

MAGIC STEALS

MAGIC SHIFTS

MAGIC STARS

MAGIC BINDS

MAGIC TRIUMPHS

The Iron Covenant

IRON AND MAGIC

UNTITLED IRON AND MAGIC #2

Hidden Legacy Series

BURN FOR ME

WHITE HOT

WILDFIRE

DIAMOND FIRE

SAPPHIRE FLAMES

EMERALD BLAZE

RUBY FEVER

Innkeeper Chronicles Series

CLEAN SWEEP

SWEEP IN PEACE

ONE FELL SWEEP

SWEEP OF THE BLADE

SWEEP WITH ME

Kinsmen

SILENT BLADE

SILVER SHARK

THE KINSMEN UNIVERSE (anthology with both SILENT BLADE and SILVER SHARK)

FATED BLADES

The Edge Series

ON THE EDGE

BAYOU MOON

FATE'S EDGE

STEEL'S EDGE

About the Author

Ilona Andrews is the pseudonym for a husband-and-wife writing team, Gordon and Ilona. They currently reside in Texas with their two children and numerous dogs and cats. The couple are the #1 *New York Times* and *USA Today* bestselling authors of the Kate Daniels and Kate Daniels World novels as well as The Edge and Hidden Legacy series. They also write the Innkeeper Chronicles series, which they post as a free weekly serial.

For a complete list of their books, fun extras, and Innkeeper installments, please visit their website https://ilona-andrews.com/ .

CPSIA information can be obtained
at www.ICGtesting.com
Printed in the USA
BVHW051044050223
657905BV00014B/416